Is It Enough Yet?

IS IT ENOUGH YET?

MELANCHOLIC AND MONSTROUS STORIES INSPIRED BY MILLENNIAL MUSIC

EMILY FLYNN-JONES

Is it Enough Yet?

Published by Glory Box Press
British Columbia, Canada.
gloryboxpress@gmail.com

First edition, 2024

ISBN: 978-1-989884-92-8

Cover design, interior design, and formatting by Emily Flynn-Jones.
Editing by Emily Flynn-Jones and Glory Box Press.

This is a work of fiction. Names, characters, businesses, places, events, and incidents are either the product of the author's imagination or used in a fictitious manner. Any resemblance to actual persons, living or dead, or actual events is purely coincidental.

For the songs that made me cry and
the ones that saved my life.

Content Warnings

This book contains delicate subject matter as well as depictions of violence. Content warnings for each story can be found at the end of the tale in an 'outro' section. This also includes a description of the inspiration for the story and may contain spoilers.

Contents

Rot Girl Movement

Avis felt the slight contraction and following gush while she sat in math class. She closed her eyes and inhaled as if she could hold everything else in too, but it was useless. Nothing would work. It had started and there was no going back. The longer she sat with it, the more she felt the viscous substance spread over the gusset of her once-white underwear. Considering her age, why couldn't her mom buy her underwear in literally any other color? Then the odor came. It was subtle—it started that way—a sweet scent like honey. The boy seated next to her sniffed at the sweetening air and looked at her. He knew. Squirming slightly trying to redirect liquid that was threatening to trickle to her thigh, she raised a reluctant hand. The entire class turned to look at her. They knew. Of course, they did. She was thirteen and a half, after all, she was late, and it was her time. There would be only one girl left in class now, Cass, and she'd stay alone that way until graduation. The teacher simply nodded his head, silently handed her the hall pass and nodded to Oliver

Pang in the front row, who sped his way to the office to inform on Avis's status. Soon the masked and gloved janitor would be in to remove her chair. Avis followed Oliver out the door with as much dignity as someone trying to squeeze their cervix for dear life can muster—the amount being zero.

In the bathroom, she enters the end stall and takes her uniform skirt down. Plopping down onto the toilet seat, she braved a look. It wasn't as bad as she had expected. What had felt like a geyser gush was actually spotting and not red. The color was a weak orange and the texture almost waxy. Then a cramp came on hard, pushing out slick clumps into the toilet. She smashed her hand against the wall of the stall to brace against the pain and let out a curse.

"Are you alright?" a sweet voice called, making Avis jump. She hadn't heard anyone come in.

"Yeah," she replied begrudgingly, unsure if she wanted this to be a sulky solitary experience or if she was glad of the company. "Not for much longer, though," she concluded, dropping her head into her hands, which put her in direct line of sight of the catastrophe coming from between her legs.

She cleaned herself up as best as she could, preparing for her walk of shame. Because she couldn't sit there forever, she somehow got her shit together enough to unlock the unit's door and step out. Greeting her was Cass, who was leaning against a sink, exhaling an astonishing amount of smoke from her vape. As Avis approached to wash her hands, Cass gestured the vape in her direction as an offering. She shook her head, no.

"Thought our final girl might want some company," Cass smiled. Avis was far from the final girl of the movies. They survived and she would not. She just shrugged in response.

"You're the final girl," Avis replied.

"Whoopie for me," Cass said, taking another long drag.

Together they made the long walk to the Principal's office, who would be expecting her along with her parents. She left tiny trails of peachy sludge and a sugary fragrance in her wake. Once the bell rang, students would flood the halls and play their usual game of fucked up hopscotch around the stains.

***

In her room, a place she will have to get used to since it is where she will languish away, her parents give her the necessities for the rot girl ritual. She is given a tin of yellow paint for her walls, plastic sheets to cover her mattress, spare sheets to replace the ones she will inevitably spoil, a pile of ancient magazines to keep her company, and reams of gauze to wrap herself in like a Mummy.

Then they confiscate her phone and computer, the only things to connect her to the outside world. Not that it mattered much. As the last rot girl, she didn't really have anyone to call. Not that she would have, anyway. Close friendships were generally discouraged because they didn't want to risk girls 'syncing up' and bringing on a swath of the rot, and pre-pubescent boys were definitely not worth hanging out with. She was utterly alone and now she was mad about it. How could this be happening to her? How could her parents be so stinking casual about it? She might have to rot, but she was gonna do it her way.

She kicked the gaslight yellow paint can only hurting herself and leaving an apricot-toned smudge of herself on the tin. If it was her fate to wither in these four walls, they would be in her style. She stomped over to the outdated CD player that she was allowed to keep and inserted her girl rock mix. There was an urge to blast it, but she didn't want to alert her parents to unapproved activities. She could still internalize the rage in the lyrics and that's the feeling she needed to sustain herself right now.

Avis began tearing the magazines to shreds. She organized the pieces by color and glued them to her walls. It was a satisfying process of destruction and reconstitution. When she was done, she had the words *'she should have died when she was born, she should have worn the crown of thorns, she should have been a son'* in massive multi-color lettering around her room. While not the words of her riot grrrl icons, the lyrics seemed appropriate for a girl to rot to.

Spent, she crashed down onto her bed with a squelch to admire her handiwork. Her mind was as consumed with the rot as her body was. Raising a hand high over her head, she noticed that it seemed a little translucent. The flesh was yellow-tinged, and she could see her blue blood vessels clearly. She felt softer all over and now that the end was nearing, she couldn't help thinking about the beginning.

***

It all started thirteen years ago when Holly Marsh had a literal meltdown. She's just celebrated her thirteenth birthday two days prior when her flow started on a park swing. The sway of her playful activity sprayed stains up and down the playground. The other kids ran screaming, leaving her to suffer alone. When her parents found her—which they did easily by following the tracks of color—she had dragged herself to the shelter of the prim and perfect trees planted to outline the children's park to match the prestige of the gated neighborhood of Honey Glades. She was a mess and making more of one as she stained the pristine green with all kinds of orange.

Instantly, it was clear this was no average period. She was shedding more than her uterine lining. The flesh on her thighs where they rubbed together was sloughing off and her pupils were a pale yellow and tearing up pus. Apparently, when she'd taken her shoes off, her socks were a ruddy amber where gloop had pooled from toenails that were detaching themselves.

A string of doctors examined her. They all agreed that she was decaying but had no cause and no cure, so she just laid alone in her bed while her insides putrefied and flowed out of her degenerating skin.

Then there was another girl, and another, and another. Sometimes a girl would just stop showing up at school and no one would ask questions. It became such a frequent event at the Middle School that they instituted the quarantine protocols. The community was locked down. No one came or went for fear of spreading the unknown disorder. It was then decided that the best course of action was to confine a rotting girl to her room where she could pass into putrescence without being of bother to the eyes of others. This was referred to as 'giving them their dignity.' They all died looking at their yellow walls and none were born to replace them. It was considered too risky. Girls in Honey Glades were a dying breed. The end of Avis would be their total extinction.

***

Thinking about it made Avis furious. Her chromosomes were not her fault. Every girl before her had just taken it lying down, literally. She would not. She was getting out.

Avis bandaged herself to leave less evidence, turned the dial on her CD player up slightly and flung her squishy legs out her second-story window. Clumsily, she turned to shimmy down the trellis, snagging her gauze—so much for leaving less trace and keeping her skin and organs in a girl shape a little longer. She dropped the last few steps, landing on her ass since her softening legs couldn't take her weight with the force.

She looked around to make sure no one had seen her embarrassment and highly illegal activity and then she asked herself, "So, what does a dead girl wanna do?"

This dead girl knew what she wanted to do.

5

***

At dusk, she found herself outside Cass's house. She circled, trying to identify her bedroom. The only upstairs room with a light on was painted yellow. *Ironic*, she thought. This had to be her room.

Avis wandered the manicured lawn looking for a rock. She found plenty in a landscaping display and took a handful. As she raised her hand to lob one at the window, she noticed was already yellow goo edging its way out of her cuticles. She shook her head at the offensive appendage and took her shot. As the small stone made contact, the noise felt thunderous against the quiet of the street. By instinct, she swivelled around looking for a place to hide but was interrupted, "Avis?" Cass looked down at her with confusion. "What the hell are you doing here?" she whispered.

"I'm rotting!" she sassed back. "What does it look like?"

"Uh," Cass replied, "I can see that."

"But, for real," Avis announced. "I'm breaking the rules. Wanna join?" Cass smiled and nodded warmly, holding up a single finger indicating for her to wait and then she disappeared back into her room and the light went out.

A few minutes later, Cass came out of her backdoor. "So," she asked, "what are we doing?"

"Whatever we want!"

When Avis said *whatever we want*, she didn't actually have a plan in mind, so she just led them aimlessly, trying to keep to the shadows of the sidewalks to be more discrete. They walked in a comfortable silence that was undertoned with the excitement of rebellion when Avis asked, "How come you have a yellow bedroom?"

Cass looked coy for a moment, dropping her head. "You'll think it's stupid," she said.

"I'm almost dead," Avis replied. "That's stupid. I swear I won't think your thing is stupid." She smiled, trying to be equally cheeky and reassuring.

"Well," Cass said, "It's, like, I don't always get treated like a girl and I'm never gonna get *that* girl experience," she continued gesturing to Avis's deteriorating body, "and it's not like I want it, for you or for anyone, but it's just another reminder that I'm different. So the yellow is me saying that I am a girl. But then it's also kind of a fuck you to all the rot shit." She paused for a moment before asking, "Does that make sense?"

"Kinda," Avis replied. "I'm not sure I totally get it, but if it makes you happy, that's cool. And I definitely like the 'fuck you' part."

They approached the old elementary school. Closed now because it was obsolete after everyone stopped breeding to prevent the rot, the gates were wrapped in locks, many broken from the exploits of those who made it to teen boredom to trespass on for all manner of miscreant behavior. Avis wanted to know what that behavior might be, so she stopped at the barred entrance with more purpose than she'd ever felt. "You wanna go in there?" she asked.

"Okay," Cass replied as Avis stomped forward and started to pull at the chains, keeping her from another thing she didn't know. Cass joined in and they slowly untangled the mess of chains, creating enough give to squeeze through the wrought gates and slip into a place of history that they were the last to know and a present totally transformed. It wasn't the intentionally sterile place they once attended and played cautiously, as their teachers told them. Now it was corrupted with erupting weeds in the cracks of concrete and the lines of wet-pour rubber that made up the majority of the grounds. This black buoyant ground was supposed to protect them and absorb the shock of any fall, but its gentle surface could do nothing for the rot and would never rot itself.

If only Avis were a rubber girl.

The windows were boarded up where stones and bricks had broken them. Avis wished there was just one clear pane of glass left for her to hurl something through to create a void for her to scream into. Rotters were always quiet. Once the process started, they disappeared, and you never heard a peep from them again, but Avis was feeling like she just found her voice, and it was brick.

As they wandered the grounds, casually kicking trash that had accumulated, it felt like a place so far removed from their carefully constructed community. The formerly characterless cream walls of the building were covered in a collage of color, featuring imagery and language Avis vaguely knew to be taboo. Printed in stylish fonts and scrawled in rushed print were phrases like: *yellow is not mellow, let them bleed, flow freely, don't shame our sugar girls, we're all already dead, Honey Glades is a hell you made.* It was like nothing she'd ever seen before, but she could tell it was riotous against the primmed, pruned and hyper-ruled town she'd known most of her life.

It was a mess. A mess like that wasn't allowed anywhere else in The Glades, and that made it glorious. Avis delighted in it, whooping and kicking a stone across the graveyard playground, smashing it into the aging entry doorway. The doors rattled and swung open slightly, letting out an almighty crack in the quiet air that made the pair shiver and reach for one another. Avis looked down, mortified that she was contaminating Cass with the sludge of her rotting hands. Quickly, their hands were disconnected from the fright of the stone coming hurling back out through the doors directly at them.

"That's not the knock, knockers." Confused glances were exchanged before the voice repeated itself.

They were both frozen, fingers barely scraping from when they'd been forced to disengage when the stone had been launched at them. "Who the heck is that?" whispered Cass.

The voice came again. Cass was backing away, ready to run. "Did you hear me or—" a boy of about fifteen poked his head through the gap in the door and paused. He looked stunned then spun on his heels running back inside the crumbling school hollering, "Holy fuck guys, there's a rotter out there!" Immediately, there was all kinds of action: excited cross-chatter and scrambling noises of feet all headed their way.

"Let's get out of here," Cass said, but it was too late. A gang of youths—some familiar, some not—came rushing through the doors to revel in the spectacle of the rot. They encircled the girls, chattering wildly with wide, curious eyes.

Avis decided she'd front like this was all cool and as if she wasn't dripping with decay all for public display.

"Yo!" said one of the unfamiliar guys, "You gonna get in here, rotter, or you looking to get us all caught?" Avis and Cass exchanged glances and followed the boys into the darkness of the building, winding corners, passing useless classrooms until they reached the centre of the maze, the assembly room. The once bright and playful place Avis remembered well, was completely transformed. It was still a playground, but perverted into a dark variant with a bevy of candles, mostly burnt-out, littered with beer cans and liquor bottles, old mattresses strewn about, and the walls covered in the passions of graffiti.

Avis and Cass were guided to the premium seats: a stinking, floral, cigarette-burned couch in the centre of the room. The boys all took their places around them—there were six of them— holding beers and puffing at joints but staring at the girls, every one of them. One of the older ones made the first move, fetching a couple of beers as an offering to them. Avis had never drunk alcohol before, but, what the heck, she was dying. She wanted to try a few things every rot girl was denied.

Avis took a generous slug on the can. The drink was a little earthy and carbonated, but not totally unpleasant. She felt the bubbles course through her with an ecstatic shiver. Next to her,

Cass sipped at hers cautiously. Before she knew it, Avis was half a beer down and feeling a lightness in her brain and body as fucks floated out of her. Feeling emboldened, she asked, "So, is this what you guys do here? Just sit and drink in silence? Doesn't seem like a ton of fun to me."

The boys exchanged glances. Eventually, a dark-haired boy with a lip-piercing and a t-shirt with a distorted smiley face broke the silence. "We've just never seen one of you, you know, out in the wild," he said.

And you never will again, Avis thought.

"Never seen the walking dead, huh?" she replied. The boys laughed awkwardly. Even Cass cracked a little smile. "Do I freak you out?"

"Nah," said another boy. He was one of the youngest and had the hood of his sweatshirt flung low, almost covering his eyes with just a pop of dirty blonde mussy hair peeking out.

"Why would we be afraid of you?" the dark-haired, pierced boy spoke again.

"It's just, like, a surprise," said the older guy who had given her the beer that was now empty. "And we ain't got nothin' to be afraid of from you," he continued. "Boys don't rot. You're the one taking all the shit."

Avis liked this answer and waved her empty can, inviting another that was thrown to her by the older boy. "Doesn't mean we're not pissed about it," a new voice spoke up. He was older, too, and wore denim that were more rip than jeans. "We're all dead too. Just in a different way."

"What do you mean?" Cass piped up, the beer clearly kicking in.

"We got no future, man," ripped jeans continued. "We're stuck here cuz of the quarantine. We'll never go nowhere or do nothin' with our lives. This is fucking it!" He declared, spreading his arms to display the ruined room.

The older one continued the thought, "No girls, no offense, Cass, so no kids—not that I want any. The town's dying with us, there's no jobs, no opportunities. We'll rot here too, just slower than you."

"That don't mean what's happenin' to you sucks any less, mind you," hoodie added.

Avis had never thought about the community. She'd been taking this whole thing personally and just dreading her turn. She'd never wanted to live more badly and wanted life for these boys even harder. Raising her beer, she said, "If this is all we got, let's do a bit of living."

A chorus of *cheers* roused from the group, and the beer and weed flowed. The more it flowed, the more noticeably comfortable Cass became, and Avis felt relaxed and loose for the first time in her short life, and not just because her body was melting.

***

She found herself sat next to the guy with the piercings. They both had a lot of thoughts and feelings about the rot. Apparently smoking opened up your mind and alcohol made you lose your inhibitions, so the conversation flowed. "Does anyone even know how long the rot lasts?" he asked. Avis shook her head. She had no idea how long was left on her decaying biological clock because they had no information. The gone girls had no funerals. As soon as they went home for that last time, they were just considered dead.

"This could be my last day on Earth as far as I know," she shrugged.

"That fucking stinks," he shook his head at her. "You're just a kid. There's so much you could have been or done." The use of the past tense didn't escape her and made her realize there was something she wanted to do before she died. Something that he could help her with.

She placed her hand on his cheek, staring into his sympathetic eyes, but quickly retracted it when she realized that her touch was sticky. She left behind a small, slimy yellow handprint on his skin. She wanted to kiss him—to kiss anyone—but now she was self-conscious despite the inebriation. He lifted some of her substance away with a finger and not with disgust, to her surprise. He raised the finger to his nose. "You smell…" there was a pause while he looked for words, "sweet." She blushed. "Have you never been kissed before?" he asked.

"No," she replied, shyly.

He leaned into her, tilting his head slightly to the left, and planted his lips on hers. It was just more than a peck, but it filled her with a new heat and as he pulled away; she inhaled to try to steady herself.

He licked his lips. "You taste delicious."

She'd just had her first kiss, and it was pleasant for them both, but her high didn't last long. She felt it in her whole body, a sort of slackening. The seat beneath her felt moist. It wasn't the types of wet she'd experienced from good dreams. The rot was accelerating. She could tell. She rose suddenly, to the boy's surprise. Everyone was looking at her but also nosing the air. She stooped to jeans boy and whispered a thank you in his ear, placing a gentle kiss on the cheek she'd already marked. She didn't have long left, and there were things she wanted to do, and the headiness of first kisses and intoxication had given her the motivation.

"Can you smell that?" The older boy asked. "You didn't bring scented candles again, did you?" He directed the question to the boy with the hood, who shook his head in vehement denial.

"I think it's her," the boy she'd kissed said.

"It's like apple pie, candy canes, lemon frosting, and cinnamon all at once," said a boy she hadn't heard from yet.

The boys narrowed in on her. They were all uncontrollably following their noses, but she didn't like the feeling of them closing in. Bursting out of the circle, she seemed to stun them out of the trance. Cass sensed her discomfort and was right behind her, protective. Avis headed to a table and grabbed a beer and a can of spray paint. She held them up and said, "Can we take these? This rotter has some more business to attend to."

There was unanimous nodding from the boys. She took Cass's hand and headed out. As they walked down the corridor, she heard one of them say, "That girl's not rotting. She's ripening."

***

They head away from their elementary school adventure, laughing and chattering while telling one another to *shush* loudly, not being very discrete for two girls on the lam. Stumbling slightly, Cass asks, "Where are we headed?"

"To the Honey Glades cemetery," Avis said.

Like most of the town, the graveyard is immaculate. It's the type of perfection that Avis has just realized to be fakery to cover up the bleakness that rots not just their girls but their entire, enclosed and excluded from the real world existence. *Like sprinkling glitter on shit*, she thought. She glanced behind her at all the peachy sludge evidence her body had left behind, and she had a moment of concern.

Then she took in the graveyard. There were nowhere near enough headstones, and it made her furious. She'd already left physical evidence behind. Now she wanted to leave a more lasting impression of her existence, as well as all the other girls who had rotted before her. Armed with the two cans they'd taken from the boys, they had everything they needed.

"What exactly's the plan?" Cass asked with a slight slur.

"We're gonna make a memorial," she said. "We're gonna make sure that everyone in this town remembers the girls that are gone and they wanted forgotten."

There had been so many over the years that they couldn't remember everyone's names, but they started with Holly Marsh, the original rot girl, and sprayed her name on a stone. Next, it was Emily Benedict. Then Amanda Long, Lacy Hamilton, Clarissa Jones, May Khan, Hailey O'Sullivan, Katie Norman,

13

Carol Turner, Wendy Fitzgerald, Sara Cox, Melody Mann, Hannah Watson, Leah and Laura Wong; the list went on. Her actions might be considered sacrilege, but she could only see justice as she painted every fresh letter.

They ran out of paint and memories, eventually. They took a break, laying, legs entwined and breathless from rebellion on the perfectly green grass that surrounded the graves. They'd done a lot, but it wasn't enough and wasn't for everyone.

"How are you doing?" Cass asked. Avis couldn't remember the last time anyone had asked her that because she was so temporary that it didn't matter to anyone.

"I'm..." she had to think. "I'm nearly done," she said, honestly.

She was fatigued. She could feel the liquescence of her body starting to bog her down. Part of her wanted to stay here until the end—and parts of her would—but there was one more thing she wanted to try. "I wanna get out of here," she said.

"Sure," Cass replied. "Where to?"

"No," she corrected. "Out of this town."

"That's impossible," Cass returned. "We're walled in. There's guards at the gates and everything." She shook her head with sadness. "No one's ever gotten out."

"But has anyone tried?" Avis said back.

***

They had to move much more slowly now. Avis's skin was almost transparent at this point, fingernails were sliding off her every few hundred yards, she felt pus behind her eyes and they were loose in her head which made for dizzying movement.

"What are you gonna do if out get out?" Cass asked.

"Don't you mean what are *we* gonna do *when* we get out?" she replied. Cass just smiled empathetically at this. In truth, Avis had no answer. She'd never been a dreamer. What was the point in the dead dreaming? Her limited education hadn't given her the tools to imagine a life. She decided to turn the question on her new and only friend.

Cass had answers. She wanted gender-affirming surgery, to meet other trans people for a feeling of acceptance, to travel to places where the sun always shined and she could swim in the ocean, to go to university and do something with libraries because she loved to read and escape into different worlds and learn all the many everythings they had to teach us, to fall in love, maybe even get her heart broken. There was so much Cass wanted, so much she deserved and would never get. Avis blessed her lack of imagination because at least she hadn't lived with that pain of the never-evers.

Trudging so slowly now, Avis could feel her body shrinking with every step. She wished every dream could come true for Cass. A dying wish. Surely she was allowed that.

Finally, they approached the North-East gate that led to reality. As expected, security guards monitored it, but there were many more people there, Avis's parents included. The adventure was over, as was her life. "I'll distract them," Avis whispered. "You make a run for it."

Cass didn't make a move. They walked together, towards inevitability.

***

Approaching the crowd, Avis realized that it was comprised of every parent who had lost a girl to the rot. They all looked furious, but something else as well... hungry? Her body had putrified to such a state that she collapsed in front of the crowded adults of Honey Glades. It felt like giving up, but she had no choice. She was who she was, and that was a rotter.

"What do you think you were playing at?" Avis's mother growled. "You were told the rules."

"Just some mild juvenile delinquency," she managed to puff out.

15

No one seemed impressed with this answer, nor did they seem to hear it. They were all in some sort of daze, heads aloft, inhaling the air deeply.

"She's ready," one of the group announced.

The adults strode toward her in a coordinated rhythm, their whispers of sweet treats filling the air: cherries, marzipan, star anise, custard cream tarts, banoffee pie, caramel, rich fudge... then they were surrounding her.

"I can tell you've been up to no good," her mother cursed her. "You didn't last as long as the others."

How long did the others last?

"The sin makes her all the sweeter," Mrs Watson said, lapping at her lips.

They were on her in unison. She was aware of someone suckling at her stomach, others nibbling at her shoulders and neck, while another tore into her fingers. She felt little pain, mostly the popping and splurging of her innards as they putrified. The sounds of sucking and munching as they devoured her were grotesque. She opened her eyes while they remained and saw Cass. Her friend looked torn between making a break for the exit and joining in the carnage. Avis just nodded her head, giving her permission for whatever she wanted to do. Then she closed her eyes for the last time and endured the feasting sounds until the end.

When the crowd cleared, they'd consumed the sugar and spice of her body, leaving only the sinful heart, because that's what girls are made of.

Outro

Should this story be directly inspired by one of the many superb and inspiring riot grrrl bands of the third-wave feminist movement? Probably. I'm sorry, Bikini Kill, L7, Babes in Toyland, Bratmobile, Sleater-Kinney and co. You were so critical to my coming to understand my feelings about being a girl in the world and the inequities we face and you fit so with spunk and a no-fucks fashion that I will forever be in awe of. It really was a moment in music and movement in culture that is worth memorializing. You can still feel/hear their reverbs today in bands like Sweeping Promises, Wet Leg, Cherry Glazer, The Sonder Bombs and many more. But, it was Placebo's lyric: "Since I was born I started to decay, now nothing ever, ever goes my way" from *Teenage Angst* that brought this dystopian world to life where girls are afflicted by what society deems an essential part of 'girlness'—bleeding. Lead singer, Brian Molko's gender presentation—radically androgynous for the '90s—and sexual orientation also had a significant influence on the way that gender is used in the story.

To be clear, I am no gender essentialist and rock an intersectional feminism with awareness of privileges that make me a dedicated life-long learner when it comes to my blindspots and unconscious biases. But gender essentialism is what plagues this fictional town. It is the 'bad guy.' And I hope I injected the story with my earliest learnings from third-wave feminism and the music idols that spawned it: that this world will eat girls alive if we let it.

Help I'm Alive

There are four stages to swallowing.

One: The oral stage. This takes place in the mouth as the eater chews. The eater is in control of the swallowing process at this phase. The tongue then moves the softened food to the back of the mouth and the soft palate rises to block off the channel to the nasal passages. From here, the process is involuntary.

Two: The pharyngeal stage. As the food reaches the back of the throat, a reflex is triggered. This causes the pharynx to contract, which pushes the food downwards. At the same time, the epiglottis folds to cover the trachea, which, cleverly, prevents food from passing into the airway.

Three: The esophageal stage. Now there is only one route for the food: down the esophagus. As the food moves down this tube-like organ, the lower esophagus sphincter (yes, we have over 50 types of sphincters in our bodies) relaxes, which allows it to pass into the stomach.

Four: The gastroesophageal stage. With the food having entered the stomach, the sphincter contracts to prevent reflux, or acids escaping into the throat, and the stomach starts the process of digestion.

This is just supposed to happen. It is an automatic, mostly involuntary process.

But not for me. What I have is called psychogenic dysphagia. Making it all in my head and utterly my fault, or so I'm led to believe by the complete lack of support and empathy I get from doctors and the only person in my life who knows, my husband Zahid. As a lawyer, he thinks we can logic our way out of this, but I can't just put my defective body on trial. I have to treat it kindly and do the hard work with my psychiatrist and speech-language pathologist to find the cause and then the cure for my unusual affliction.

Initially, I could still chew. I quite liked that part since it comes with all the flavors and textures—the interesting part of food. Everything after that just doesn't work. In the early days of this issue, I would put tiny amounts of my favorite foods into my mouth and chew. I was careful to restrict the food to my incisors and canines so there was no chance of the stuff passing to the back of my mouth and risking a failed swallowing scenario which always induce panic attacks and even fainting. Then I would spit out the food once all the taste was taken from it. Eventually, I became more and more afraid that reflex would worm food back to my molars and dangerously near a swallow.

It was all too traumatic and disgusted my husband, so I abandoned the exercise even though the doctors said this would be a good recovery practice for me.

Now, I find the idea of swallowing equal parts frightening and disgusting, frankly, so I have not put anything in my mouth for seven months for fear of triggering my faulty swallow system. I can't take in solids or liquids, which is not healthy for the human body. The pounds were falling off of me and I was dangerously dehydrated. This forced an extreme move, and I must receive my hydration and nutrients intravenously. It is not particularly attractive, but it keeps me alive, and I suppose that is something, but I do have to deal with the show-off, masticating masses all the time and most intimately at dinner parties such as tonight.

My husband's work colleagues are dinner party fiends. I find myself at a table full of feasting fucks almost every other week where I am expected to perform normative acts of eating by pushing my food around my plate, feeding Zahid like sickening new sweethearts, feigning an allergy, delicately claiming tummy troubles, or whatever I can come up with if my non-eating is observed. Honestly, no one gives Amy shit about her vegetarianism, and everyone takes Rita's diet phases—keto, pagan, Atkinson's, etc.—seriously. Why can't I just be a non-eater? They chose their restrictions. I did not. But we don't talk about it because it is shameful and weird. Instead, I'm forced to choke down compliments on how great I look, invasive questions from Kelly about my diet and exercise regime, and the judgmental whispers of 'anorexia.' Each time I endure this shit is an emotional setback and makes me feel smaller than the size 2 I have been reduced to.

At these feeding affairs, I fake fineness until it hurts. I'm surrounded by people who fail to see or understand that there is something wrong, and by obscene amounts of cuisine that I find frightening and offensive. Being at a dinner table is like a prison, and I have to try to tune out the disgusting sounds of chewing, utensils scraping against plates, lips smacking, groans produced by the pleasure of taste, and all the compliments to the chef who is the asshole responsible for the nightmare scenarios I repeatedly find myself in.

Tonight we were at the Roth's, where it was commented that we never host anymore. It is a thinly veiled criticism. Someone says that they miss my matar paneer. Another craves my dal makhani. There's a collective fond reminiscence of my lamb tikka and samosas, so moreish people barely had room for their entrée. Zahid wraps a loving-looking arm over my shoulders and says that we are simply teasing their tastebuds and whetting their appetites. Karen Roth twists this into an invitation for one month from now since we have the Manning's potluck for Super Bowl in a fortnight. I smile through gritted teeth I'm afraid will break since they have brittled with my condition. I have a month to dread being their reluctant host.

Since I have not been eating, I have not been cooking much either. It's not as though I've lost the talent, but rather the taste for it. Why would I labour over something that I cannot partake in? Zahid is a busy man who often works late and has been relatively content with the meal delivery kits service we subscribed to, but he often laments the days of home-cooked meals. I also work and was never a meal-making machine anyway, but our current freezer full of ready-made dishes won't make the cut for a potluck or hosting a full menu event. This leaves me with the anxiety of not one but two forthcoming cooking extravaganzas looming over me, and I confront Zahid in the car on the way home for not helping protect me from these situations. His sympathy must be wearing thin—that or the Scotch has eroded his empathy, since he simply shrugs and notes that I don't have to eat the food, I just have to make it.

***

The dreaded Super Bowl Sunday is upon us and with revulsion I do the grocery shopping to acquire the ingredients for a massive chicken biriyani. It is straightforward to make and will serve as a side dish that won't clash with the varied dishes other wives have signed up to bring. I have not set foot in a supermarket in at least six months. The stacked shelves mock me and each time I pick up a required item, it's like a kick in my empty gut. Seeing people with overflowing carts makes me nauseous. I escape this torture chamber as quickly as possible.

Preparing the meal is no better. Every step is part of a new pre-swallowing stage that I have invented, which sickens and scares me. In my anxious state, I am not paying proper attention and slice my finger open while cutting the poultry. By instinct, I raise my finger to my mouth as I hurry to the sink. But there I stop. I realize I've been sucking my own blood and imbibing it. I feel the four stages at work in my body. It's slightly painful, as muscles are that have not been exercised in a while, but I do it. I swallow. I'm not stopping either. I stare at my reflection in the kitchen window as I suck my wound clean. When there is no longer any liquid on my tongue or metallic taste on my buds, I pulled my finger from my suddenly hungry mouth and look at it. The cut is deep but clean. I wash and bandage it before going back to my cooking with some confusion. My achievement in swallowing and the blood—especially the blood—make the cooking process tolerable, somehow, and before I know it, I've made my first dish in months.

The biriyani is met with approval from Zahid's workmates, and I'm grateful that at a casual serve-yourself event like this, I don't have to work so hard to hide my non-eating. I carry around an empty plate as though I've eaten my fill. The afternoon flies by. Someone wins the game. I don't tell my husband that I managed to do the impossible—swallow—and I think about blood.

***

I know I will try to swallow again, but I have to ensure the conditions are right. I try water, yogurt, and juice, all the soft and 'simple' things my doctors recommended, but nothing goes down. They only induce panic attacks as stage two fails and I'm left choking, spluttering, and unnerved. It becomes clear what the missing piece is—blood.

If I'm going to do this, I have to be careful. I can't just show up with cuts on me, so I devise a 'rehearsal dinner' to serve to Zahid, which allows me to have another 'accident' during preparation. This time, I start with my 'famous' samosas and slice off a piece of my thumb while peeling the potatoes. With excitement and intention, I become overzealous and carve out the thinnest flap of skin. There is much more blood this time, and I suck at it eagerly. It goes down velvety smooth, even though every organ involved in the gross mechanics of swallowing play its part. The blood hits my long-empty stomach with a welcome warmth. But when the blood is done, I am not.

22

The flap of skin teases at my tongue. Without thinking, I tear it away with my teeth and let it venture into my mouth. The temptation to chew takes me and I follow it. It's such a petite morsel. The sliver of flesh breaks down into the most minuscule pieces. Perhaps I can manage it? I tongue the bits back in my mouth, and it slides down as it should. I am exhilarated and pleased that I am making progress with my disorder, however strangely.

It's miraculous. After months, I can eat, but only myself. I'm not personally concerned that I don't feel revolted by it. I am, however, concerned with concealing it because I know others will find it repulsive, and I have no intention of stopping. I feel my healing era coming on.

***

I take up cooking again to cover up the wounds that sustain me. But I can't fake daily clumsiness in the kitchen, or it might draw some attention, so I find ways of creating and consuming hidden wounds. The primary difficulty is my need to reach my cuts with my mouth in regions that no one will notice during these sweaty summer months of short sleeves and skirts. More challenging will be leaving my husband oblivious to scabs and scars during our intimate moments.

Years of yoga come in handy. I make tiny slits between my toes and bend and contort my body to meet the lacerations with my lips. I got the idea from the representation of drug users on the hospital procedurals I devour, unlike food. Zahid and I always make love in the dark, so I start to make small slices on the sides of my breasts, cupping them and bringing them to my mouth to nurse at the blood. My husband and I are sharing meal times again, he just doesn't know it. Every few days, I carefully carve a thin layer of skin from a fingertip. Only enough to burst the capillaries beneath and bring blood to the surface. The meat is so fine it melts in my mouth, easily passing the four stages of swallowing. They heal quickly, and from the bandaids, my husband assumes that I am simply relearning my culinary craft after a long break.

By the time the night of our party arrives, I have a set of five mildly mutilated digits. Looking at the regrowth, my fingerprints are gone. The markers of my former identity have been erased and replaced by the new eater I have become. It is the first time I have had to dress up in a while, and the wired bra bites at my healing breasts, while the strappy, heeled sandals make my slashed toes sting. But the pains are just reminders of my tasty triumph against the dysphagia that was slowly making me perish into skin and bones while eating away at my mental fortitude and confidence. I was disappearing, and no one noticed or cared. The psychological condition that rendered me incapable of swallowing was a cry for help that went unheard. I may be literally eating myself now, but it is on my own terms, and that is a delicious power and form of control that I thought I had lost forever. The more I take in of myself, the more myself I will become.

Outro

Content warnings: Disordered eating, auto-cannibalism

I have battled disordered eating for the best part of twenty years. My issues are swallowing-related and this is something that is quite misunderstood, making it difficult to get the right kind of support. But all forms of disordered eating are devastating and eat the person who suffers from them alive. Inspired by this life-devastating fact and *Help I'm Alive* by Metric with its lyrics like: "They're gonna eat me alive," and "I get whatever I need, while my blood's still flowing," this sick, cannibalistic snapshot of complex relationships to food was formed.

Is It Enough Yet?

Monday, July 15th, 1822 - The Evening Post
On Saturday, July 13th, 1822, Mary Morgan was found violently beaten in her home. A suspect was taken into custody but not charged. The 26-year-old was pregnant and unwed at the time of her death.

Monday, September 23rd, 1973 - The Evening Post
Georgia Williams and Polly Hughes were found strangled Saturday night in their rental property in Neath. They are assumed to have hitchhiked home after a night out in Swansea. Police are interested in speaking to the person who picked them up, as they may have information critical to solving this brutal double murder.

Thursday, February 17th, 2011 - The Evening Post
Rebecca Wallace, aged 47, was shot and killed by her stalker ex-boyfriend in her Neath residence last night. Ms. Wallace had made numerous complaints to the police about her harasser and had a restraining order in place. The man has been arrested and charged.

In number 6 Levenfield Street, no one can hear you scream, apparently. Despite the paper-thin pre-war terrace walls, and a street of curtain-twitchers and gossipers—not to mention the fact that number 6 could hear the activities of numbers 5 and 7 with great clarity. Everyone knew that bad things went on in the house—and had done for a long time—but the facts were relayed in whispers and never rallied into any sort of action.

It was not a happy home. Not now. Not ever. Sadness and horror lived in its old bones. Some homes are alive with the laughter of loving families, dinner conversation about how days went, and the gentle snores of peaceful sleep. Other places pulse with a vile kind of life, with seeds so deep and slithering, seething shoots that hook themselves to a place like a horrendous hug. Number 6 was in such a sick embrace when Hailey and Adam moved in. It was the only place they could afford in this economy and the price was shockingly low for the neighborhood. As millennials, they pooled every possible resource and snapped up the real estate they were told would always be denied to them. The signs of rot were there from the first night, when Hailey broke something while unpacking and the berating began. The list of her wrongs was long, according to Adam. It was one of those spiraling, sprawling arguments and by the end, she couldn't even remember the originating offense. As usual, Hailey sat trying not to look gloomy—one of her most repeated crimes—until Adam ran out of bluster and demanded she get out of his sight.

With pleasure, she thought, dashing upstairs to the bathroom. She went there instead of to their bedroom because she knew she needed to cry the lightning she'd been holding in for the last forty minutes. She would need to clean herself up afterward because Adam didn't like to see weeping girls—*I'll give you something to cry about*—and she didn't want to give him the satisfaction of knowing how much his words had wounded.

Hands planted on the granite countertop, her body convulsed with quiet sobs. Not quite cried out, but exhausted from the move and the argument, Hailey raised her head to face herself in the mirror. Her eyes were puffy and bloodshot and mascara ran down her flush cheeks. She looked quite the ugly mess that he always described her to be. Staring dead at her reflection, she started to repeat all the terrible things he'd said about her. She had his anger in her and was letting it rip on herself, hurling insults like some self-harming mantra when the lights began to flicker. She heard Adam curse from downstairs and wondered how this would be her fault. Perhaps her period or her miserable face affected electricity somehow? It didn't matter how ridiculous, he would find a way to spin the blame in her direction. She'd also find a way to believe it.

Sighing, she knew it was time to clean herself up. They hadn't finished unpacking and she couldn't find the cleansing balm that would remove all traces of the bleeding mascara. Instead, she scrubbed as best she could with hand soap, digging her fingers hard into her closed eyes, trying to wash away the emotional evidence. Finished, she looked up at the vanity mirror to examine her work. With eyes blurry from the water and abrasive rubbing, she sees something strange.

It is not her reflection.

Hailey leapt back in shock as four faces stared back at her. One of the blurred bodies pointed at her and started moving her hand. As she did, words appeared all over the room, reading: "You're one of us."

She grabbed a hand towel, dabbed the water from her face and returned to the mirror, but the women were still there. It hadn't been her fuzzy eyesight. She slid down the vanity, watching more of the same ominous words etched into the walls. She traced a finger over one of the instances. It had no substance, but it was there, nonetheless. What the fuck was happening and how was she going to explain the damage to Adam? Another flickering of the lights and they steadied. Once all was illuminated again, the writing was gone, and Hailey braved another look in the mirror. The four women had disappeared, and she was alone apart from the man bashing at the bathroom door, asking what she was doing in there and accusing her of wasting water.

***

Hailey spent the next few days unpacking and dressing the house, but not well or fast enough for Adam's liking. She was never enough and never did enough. The whole time she thought she caught glimpses of feminine forms in reflective surfaces out of the corner of her eye, but when she turned to look head-on, there was nothing. She felt like she was going mad and the words, *you're one of us,* kept running through her mind and randomly appearing scrawled on walls around the house. She was certain she was going mad, and Adam was getting madder with her, in his own way.

With every argument she had with Adam, the presence of the figures and the feeling that came with them grew stronger. Faces were in the television, flashed in windowpanes, and warped in the metal of the kitchen sink. They were watching her. Adam watched her, too. His vigilant eyes waited for any invitation for another blazing row while the others watched her for reasons unknown. There was nowhere that she was free from gaze, and she felt she couldn't look anywhere.

Hailey did have to look, though. There was one point of each day where she couldn't avoid the reflections, during her required morning skincare and make-up regime. She'd tap at the mirror and quietly plead with them not to manifest. She had to keep a full face and a certain level of appearance for Adam, even though she spent most of her time locked up in their new home, doing chores. He insisted that she not, 'let herself go'.

29

Sometimes it was the bruises that insisted her make-up application. Adam would approve her look before he went to work. No matter how she presented herself, his reaction was lackluster. The reflections always left her alone while she completed her routine, but would appear the moment Adam was gone to shake their heads at her and ghost graffiti over her walls, always writing: "Is it enough yet?"

It was enough. They were making her feel like she was losing her mind.

***

Hailey was lying in bed after enduring the apology sex Adam frequently felt he was owed and trying to take her mind off the whole day by opening her eReader to a transportive romance. Something that modeled what she wanted and not what she had. Adam was making fun of her for her trashy taste, telling her she'd be a lot smarter and more interesting if she read a classic or two—as though he'd read a book in his life—when the lights went out. He cursed and immediately accused her of forgetting to top up the electricity meter. Despite her vehement denials, he aggressively elbowed her in the ribs, got up, turned on the torch mode on his phone, and marched downstairs to check. She stared at her eReader, unable to focus on the words. All she could do was worry about what a night in complete darkness with him meant for her.

That was when they appeared.

The four women were framed in the grey of her reader screen. She allowed herself to look at them properly for the first time because they were not as scary as Adam was right now.

One appeared to be in her forties with modern asymmetric bobbed hair. Two looked like late teens from the '70s with heavily feathered hair, one wearing a tube top and the other a wrapped halter top that suggested a sparkle even on the full screen. The last woman had an up-do with tendrils draping to frame her face. She wore a peasant-style dress and while seemingly in her twenties, was most certainly the oldest of the four in terms of era.

Hailey's eyes were glued to the screen, and she watched as the women's lips moved, but no sound came out. The women appeared to become flustered and were gesturing wildly at one another. The eldest woman raised her hands in a 'stop' signal before turning to face Hailey and holding up a single finger telling her to wait and then they disappeared. Her eReader was blank. She tapped at it and shook it, trying to bring it back to life. Suddenly, text started to appear.

> You're one of us.
> Look for us.
> Georgia, Polly, Rebecca and Mary.
> Look for us…
> And we'll look out for you.

"What do you want from me?" Hailey replied, more loudly than she had intended.

"What the fuck did you just say to me?" Adam asks, walking back into the room as the lights come back on.

Looking down, there were just the romantic words of her book filling her screen, and Hailey had no response. At least, none that Adam would want to hear.

*****

Adam's moods were darkening and coming more frequently. His ire and aggression were aimed at her daily now. She tried being quiet, but he accused her of being sullen and sulky for no reason. So, she started to spend time while doing her daily housework devising innocuous topics of conversation. Each was a failure. Either she blathered too much and should shut her stupid mouth, or he would do it for her, or she was awarded the dishonor of being the world's most boring human who was lucky that she found someone to put up with her. There was no right way for her to exist, though she barely did anyway.

***

Hailey did not work. When she and Adam first met, she had a job at a psychiatric ward which she loved and truly felt like she was helping people, in ways she didn't seem able to help herself. But he persuaded her to give it up since they only had one car, and the hospital was too far for transit from the new house. Besides, he wanted a better-kept home. He'd always complained about mess and disappointing meals when she'd worked and come home too exhausted for chores or culinary flare. They couldn't afford to be a single-income household, especially with the mortgage, but it was another argument she had somehow lost, disoriented in his strange reasoning. She missed her colleagues but understood they were too busy with important work to keep in touch. Now her days were deathly silent, contrasting the raucous rows of each night. They were also deeply dull, filled with thankless housework and dodging the reflective surfaces where her reflection women hid.

If Hailey had to go somewhere, she walked. Inevitably, she encountered men along the way. Men who cat-called because of how Adam made her dress. Each time, it made her feel small and guilty knowing that Adam would fly off the handle if he ever found out. Then there were the guys who told her to smile. She couldn't and she wouldn't. There was nothing to smile about. This made venturing out almost as bad as staying in, but today she had to go. After the move, their cupboards were practically empty, so she made the long walk to the grocery store. On the way back, heavy with bags of store-brand goods to match their budget, she had to pass through the Churchyard just down their road. It was in disrepair and covered in scaffolding. The grounds were overgrown, and a few headstones lined the pathway. One in particular caught her attention. It was taller than the rest, more ornately decorated, and older by a long way.

Weatherworn, some of the text obscured, but the words across the top, carved large and in capital letters: "MURDERED." Dropping her bags, she read the rest.

In loving memory of Mary Morgan.

Although the savage murderer escaped for a season the detection of man, yet God hath set his mark upon them either for time or eternity and the cry of blood will assuredly pursue him to certain and terrible but righteous judgment.

Mary. The name was common but had another resonance with her. Her reflected women had told her to look for them and mentioned a Mary. She had an odd feeling she could not shift that this was no coincidence. Looking more carefully at the damaged stone, she saw that the poor woman was killed in 1822 at the age of 26. She pictured the girl in the peasant dress. Could they be the same Mary? A shiver ran down her spine as though someone walked over her grave while she stood at another's.

She'd first encountered Mary in the mirror, just like the legend of Bloody Mary. She and her friends had told the scary story at slumber parties when they were teens and dared one another to go to the mirror and summon her. No one ever did. From what she remembered, seeing Mary in the mirror meant certain death. She already thought she was losing her grip since they started haunting her, now she felt fear and wasn't sure she could handle seeing them again.

***

Once home, she decided to make something extravagant for dinner to treat Adam. It might put him in a good mood and lead to a night without altercation. She avoided reflective surfaces while she worked. She would usually watch something on her tablet while she prepared food, but she didn't want to risk the reflection of the screen. Instead, she directed the smart home device to tune into a radio station.

Trying not to think about blood or Marys, she chopped an onion. The sharp knife gleamed. Her eyes started to water and the radio station glitched with static. Tossing the onion into a hot pan, she shouted commands into the air to return to the original station. The device spoke back, but not in its usual robotic tone. This was the voice of a frantic human woman. "Look at us," the voice pleaded. Hailey looked around her, everywhere but the window and sink where she'd seen the women before. "Look at us!" the voice called again. She knew it was the mirror women speaking to her, so she carefully picked up the smart device, examining it. It was plastic and reflected nothing. "The knife," the voice said this time.

Hailey hesitantly looked down at the implement in her hand. There they were, clear as day, even through her stinging, weepy eyes. Their presence in the blade reminded her of how dangerous this may be, and she dropped the knife on the counter. They were still in view.

"About time," one of the younger women said, her speech punctuated with a blast of a song.

The women continued to speak but were frequently disrupted by bursts of radio. Hailey was able to catch the gist, though. They were saying that she looked for and found one of them and now she should know that it meant she was going to become one of them. The words implied death, just like her Bloody Mary thesis. But, even with the audio distortion, she didn't catch anything threatening in their tone. Then one of the younger ones said, "She should just take this knife and shove it in him. Then she won't become one of us."

Staring at the knife in question, Hailey could see the last words came from the older lady. "We're breaking up... because he's coming... keep looking... find us... you'll believe... be quick..."

The radio returned to the station, playing a pop song that clashed completely with the eerie encounter seconds ago. Hailey picked up the knife again and thought about what the young one had said. Did they want to kill her? If so, why were they toying with her and not just cutting to the chase? Or did they want her to kill?

Her thoughts were interrupted by the slam of the door and Adam yelling, "What the fuck is burning?" Hailey removed the ruined onions from the stove and any chance of a peaceful evening along with them.

***

Hailey was being haunted by death—possibly her own. Rebecca was the only name she could remember from the list that the reflections had given her. She needed to find out who she was. There was one thing she knew for certain: Rebecca was dead, just like Mary. While she should have been vacuuming every nook and cranny and deep-cleaning the bathroom, she searched on her phone for Rebecca. She did not have the greatest search terms:

Rebecca dead
Rebecca ghost
Rebecca murdered

This yielded nothing because it yielded too much. Millions of hits. Far too much to scroll through. She needed to narrow the parameters. The short communications with the reflections hadn't given her much information. It was all so cryptic: *look for us, we'll look after you, you're one of us.* She remembered she'd already found one of them just down the street. She was a local girl, so she refined her search for local deaths of Rebeccas. Again, there were too many hits to review. Nervously, Rebecca added 'murder' to the search criteria and the top hit was everything and more that Hailey had dreaded. The familiar bobbed woman's face was on her screen again, this time in full color and smiling in a photograph with the headline, "Local Hairdresser Murdered in Her Home by Ex." She had lost her life in 2011. Hailey's street was named as the location of the tragedy and further digging revealed an article with police tape surrounding her house. Rebecca had lost her life, violently, within the walls where she now sat.

Hailey continued to search for murders at her address. Immediately, the gorgeous young faces of the other two girls filled the page as she scrolled furiously. Georgia and Polly were roommates in the residence in 1973 when they were brutally slain by a man who had only recently been identified by DNA. He was deceased and would not see justice, but it was assumed that one of the girls had invited him home with them after a night out.

She dropped her phone, despondent. Her neat, hard-earned home was bathed in invisible blood. She started to weep for the women of number 6 and their horrible fates. The television screen flickered on in front of her and the women were there. Not in the crispy clear resolution of their LED screen, but with the fuzz of old terrestrial television. "Now you see," said Mary, speaking for the first time.

"I see, and I'm sorry," Hailey sobbed. "But I don't know what this has to do with me." This response was met with a collective sigh.

"We were all killed here by wicked men," said Georgia.

Hailey shook her head, denying the understanding growing in her.

"His rage summoned us," Rebecca added, "because he is a wicked man, too."

"Rotten piece of shit," said Polly.

"You found us," Rebecca said. "You know the truth. The truth of us and your... situation..."

The channel suddenly changed, and for once, Hailey didn't want the reflections to be gone. She grabbed the remote control, switching channels in search of them, until finally finding them on 204.

Rebecca continued her speech. "You are one of us, but we hope you don't have to be. You just have to get out…"

Then she was gone again, replaced by some nonsense daytime TV with four chatty women. They were not her women. Hailey flipped through the channels frantically, but they were nowhere to be found. Muttering to herself about the impossibility of her situation, she didn't hear Adam come in.

"Having another productive day, I see," he said.

His chastising continued, but Hailey only caught some of it because she was still glued to the television, looking for her reflections. He screamed about working his ass off all day while she did nothing, how he sacrificed so they could have this life, that she wasn't dressed properly, and that he found her repulsive.

None of it resonated like usual because she was stuck on the words of her mirror women as it sank in how easily she might be one of them. Adam aggressively ripped the remote control from her hand, turning off the TV and flinging the controller across the room, where it shattered. Her fault, even though she didn't throw it.

The lights started to flicker.

Things spiraled quickly then. Her life flashed before her like a montage, cut to the rhythm of the lights. *Look what she made him do*. And all the things she made him do next. He dragged her up by her hair. He was in her face, his spittle spraying. He pulled her to the kitchen, tearing her sleeve. *Let me make it easy on you*. Food was slammed onto the counter for her to prepare. *Do I have to do everything?* He grabbed a pot, smashing her across the face with it before putting it onto the stove and lighting the burner. Drawers crashed open and closed. The knife landed on the counter.

It's him or her.

It's not him because she was one of them.

***

Hailey of woke in a familiar but skewed space. She was in her home, but everything was flipped around and rotten. Not rotten—burned. It felt wrong, but also peaceful and quiet. The four women surround her, reflections no more. Mary stroked her forehead, looking at her with deep sorrow. Georgia and Polly held tight to each other, one of them crying.

"I'm so sorry," says Rebecca.

Hailey can't remember the last time someone said sorry to her. "Where am I?" she asks.

"You're one of us now," Mary replied.

Dead. She knew that. "Is this Heaven or is it Hell?" she asked

"No idea," said Polly. "We're just here. Stuck in a mirror world of our death scene."

"The backwards world of living-dead girls," Georgia said.

Hailey looked around her new backwards world, where her old home was a charred crime scene obscuring her blood, which surely decorated the kitchen floor.

They turned her away and explained that they think they are guardians, watching over the house for violent activity. That is when they can make contact, because cruelty conjured them. They try to communicate with the inhabitants of the house when they sense danger—which they always do—but they have minimal means to do so. They described the house as a beacon for brutality. Often, their presence scared the women they tried to help, as they had unnerved Hailey. This could even exacerbate the situation as they watched distressed women expressing themselves to men with no tolerance for hysterics. Overall, they had managed to save a few. Others perished and joined their reflection ranks or simply disappeared.

"But the place is gone," Hailey said. "It's ashes. It's over."

"They'll rebuild," Mary says. "It's happened before. This is the place, but not the house I died in. It's as if there is a darkness here that always finds a way to survive and thrive off of death."

"So, we stay here," Rebecca said, "and we save the next one."

One of them now, Hailey was filled with a purpose in death she never found in life. She would work with these women and apply the practices of care she learned from her time at the hospital to make for a more comforting presence and warmer ways of communicating. They would work hard to become the support these endangered women needed and stop the perpetuating violence. Her ghost would leave this wretched place better than she found it, because it was enough already.

Outro

Content warnings: Domestic abuse, dubious consent, violence against women, microaggressions against women, murder of women by men.

Perhaps, the only hopeful story in this collection, this titular tale is inspired by *Heaven/Hell* by Chvrches and the repetition of the question: "Is it enough yet?" in the broader context of confusion regarding mediated messaging. This is why we have our benign Bloody Mary-type figures trying to communicate with our protagonist about the danger she is in; danger that she knows and feels but can't quite believe. (Dis)Belief being another theme in the song.

The house of undead girls is a nod to the house I grew up in. For me, it was an unhappy, unhealthy and unsafe environment until my abuser left when I was 15. At which point the place became host to an endless slumber party for other girls who were struggling at home. I hated that place and ran for the hills, never looking back, as soon as I could.

Then a friend reached out to tell me there had been a murder next door to my childhood home. I was furious, knowing there would have been signs and sounds. People would have known what went on in that home as they did with me and, yet, no one intervened. The conversation took a turn, however, as my friend spoke of my old home as a 'haven' for her in some of her hardest times. I couldn't reconcile her memories with my nightmare recollections, but then I sat with her feelings and realized something: as teens, we, without knowing, created a safer space for ourselves. That is why instead of the unusual malevolent mirror spirits, I created the living-dead girl support group. Like us, they don't know what they are doing, but they are trying to end the cycle of abuse with what they've got, which is each other, and that's a lot. They may not be the damsels who save themselves that the song speaks of, but they are standing together and saying they've had enough.

The murder stone in the story really existed and I was obsessed with it. Located in a graveyard across the street from me, I did morbid little etchings and lots of research on the case. The stone itself is unusual. It is not a headstone, and the victim is not buried beneath it. Rocked by the violence, it was created by the community a year after her death as a warning to the perpetrator that they would be watching for him and justice would be served in this life or the after.

Not All The Way

You are watering your many plants when you hear the knock on the door. It's dark out, you've not ordered anything for delivery, and no one randomly drops by anymore, at least not without a text message. You decide it's a mistake or a sales caller and ignore it.

Then the doorbell chimes. It chimes again and pairs the grating tune with a rhythmic set of raps at the door. Whoever is on the other side knows you are home because the lights are on. They might even be able to hear the trashy procedural you're blasting on the television.

Knock, knock, knock.

You're irritated now. You don't go outside. You hardly open the door unless absolutely necessary. Whoever is beckoning you outside probably doesn't know that, but it ruffles you, nonetheless. You pump up the volume on the TV just as the medical examiner is explaining the grim cause of death, and you're slightly embarrassed the outsider will know what garbage you're watching.

Bring! Knock, knock, knock, bring!

They are not giving up, so your mind runs through all the terrible things this might mean. Cops coming to tell you a loved one is deceased. A young girl in peril from some pursuer. A murderer.

You should probably stop watching these shows.

Clicking mute, you move toward your window, carefully peeling back a corner of the curtain and peeking through the gap. The front stoop is visible, but the indented doorway conceals the mysterious caller. You quickly close the curtains.

Knock, knock, knock.

The banging at the door is harder, slower, and more deliberate now. If it doesn't stop, you're going to piss off your neighbors—who already begrudgingly do a lot for you since you became housebound. They collect packages for you and redeliver them personally, so you don't have to engage with strangers, and they also text you when they go to the store to see if you need anything. You can't afford to lose the invaluable resource of their love.

You're going to have to deal with this.

You move slowly toward your front door, trying to build up courage along the way. The courage does not come.

As you reach the entranceway, there is another set of thumps to the door. The pounding is so strong, it shakes the door in its frame and makes you jump in shock. You creep forward, quietly engaging the chain lock before flipping the three thumb-turn locks and sliding the deadbolt from its latch. With a deep breath, you pry open the door as far as the chain will allow.

There is no one on your stoop.

You mutter a feeble hello into the night. There is no answer. Whoever was there must have given up, so you close the door, relieved.

But they are not gone. The bell-ringing and knocking returns, incessant this time. You whip the door open but still see no one on your steps.

What the fuck is going on?

"Hello," comes a voice from the shadow of the trees lining the sidewalk. It is a masculine voice, a little slow and slurred. Is this a drunken prank? Squinting into the dark, you can barely make out the man's shape. He is tall, and you wonder how he could have gotten back there so fast.

"I've been having a hard time watching you," he says.

You slam the door, re-secure all the locks then run to the living room, turning out all the lights and the TV so you cast no shadow to be watched. As you crouch behind the couch, familiar panic floods your mind, crushing your chest and numbing your limbs.

Your pills are in the kitchen, just through the archway of your tiny open-plan studio home. They might as well be a thousand miles away with your body going into full-on meltdown.

Your attention is drawn away from the kitchen when you hear a scraping at the window. The frightening friction moves slowly across the pane, making a grating sound that reverberates in your bones.

It's a knife. He's got a knife.

The singular shrill sound turns into a cacophony.

You see it, or them.

The street lamps cast a dim glow across the curtains, enough to illuminate thin and gnarly talons dragging down your windowpane. You close your eyes and cover your ears, trying to block out what scares your senses.

Where is your phone? You could call a neighbor at this hour, or the police. You fumble for it in the dark, but it is nowhere to be found.

Knock, knock, knock.

The eerie and intentionally measured knock sounds again, followed by scratching down the door frame. You crawl back to the front door and beg them to go away and leave you alone.

The word 'no' rides on the wind.

Then, more clearly, a raspy, "Not until you open the door."

Opening the door seems like the wrong and dangerous thing to do. Not to mention, a thing you do so rarely by the rules of your agoraphobia. But the knocking and scraping is clawing at your already delicate nerves.

You have to do something. After some fretful thought, you convince yourself you will be safe with the chain lock long enough to scream bloody murder, wake the neighborhood, and frighten off the strange and sinister man.

On shaky legs, you rise, undoing your locks and gently open the door.

He is there, again. Not in front of you, but back at the boulevard, blending in with the trees. His physique is curious. You open your mouth, but nothing comes out when you look at him. You are entranced. From what you can make out in the gloom, he's towering and wispy, with knobbly and gnarled joints. He cuts an intimidating but aged figure.

"Open the door," he requests.

"I never open the door," you say. "Not all the way."

"Tragic," he replies. He seems uncannily still. Then, occasionally, his form appears to shift with the wind, particularly his wild hair.

"What do you want?" you ask.

"I just want to waste all your time here on the sidewalk like you waste your time in there." He raises an impossibly long and lean arm, pointing to the haven that is your home.

You ask why he's been watching you.

He says it is because he cares, but you are hard to watch because he sees your life shrink and it is like witnessing someone wither and die. It seems so unnecessary to someone like him who is dying because no one cares. In fact, his situation is terminal because people hurt him. His tone is worn but has anger in it.

You almost feel pity for the peculiar man who has been terrorizing you. Almost. But that is why you are here, hidden away from the world—because of the hurt people do.

A woman walks by with her miniature dog. She gives you a quizzical look as her dog lifts its leg and urinates on the man who is talking to you, before moving on as though she didn't see or hear a thing. She is certainly not distressed, as you are. What is this man?

"You see," he says. "They don't even see me, and they treat me with no respect. That is why I am dying."

It does not seem like a reason to stalk and intimidate women to you. He is not the first man to harass you or the first to guilt-trip you about their behavior. Neither is he the first whose conduct was invisible to others.

You promised yourself you wouldn't take this shit anymore, yet here you are, in the middle of the night, indulging your tormentor. You've not only been indoors for months, your life on pause, but you haven't moved on mentally, either.

A breeze sweeps the street, making you shudder and his form sway.

You hug your robe close, finding your phone has been in your pocket this whole time. Pulling it out, you quickly snap pictures, catching eerie glimpses of him as your flash floods his hiding place in the flora.

***

You're safely locked back in your home listening to his moaning in the breeze when you open your photo app and prepare to look.

"Don't do it to yourself," he howls. "Live!" he demands, banging and scouring at the door.

You flip through the photographs, finally revealing the man. In horror, you see the gnarled, grainy, and peeling flesh of a weathered tree and, in each successive image, the unmistakable face of the man you fear—the one that keeps you caged inside—etched in the bark.

***

He continues his whining and wailing all night long. His fucked-up lullaby keeps you awake, unconsciously rocking your anxious body to its beat. But by dawn, it dies down and with the sun, dies altogether.

Is he dead like he promised?

Opening your curtains, you see it: the dead tree amidst the green. With its cracked trunk, naked branches, bent and brittle bones, and a fury of fungal growth, the tree/man is clearly dead. You call the city to have it removed, saying its rot may infect the rest of the boulevard's greenery, but really, you just don't want to have to look at him. He is no less intimidating in the cold light of day... because day and night are no different from inside.

Today is not the day you open the door all the way.

Outro

Content warnings: Stalking, agoraphobia

Call It Fate, Call It Karma is not the song from The Strokes that I would have expected to be inspired by. I was convinced a track from their phenomenal debut, *Is This It*, would be where I'd find my inspiration because I've related to its themes of disillusionment for nearly twenty-five (25) years. Listening to it on repeat, however, just transported me to my first year of university and had me dancing or feeling vaguely bummed out. A more profound darkness did not reach out to me.

I had never listened to the 2013 *Comedown Machine* record all the way through before and the last track, *Call It Fate, Call It Karma,* is such a strange one in the band's oeuvre. It gave me goosebumps. Its nostalgic, stripped-down vibes, with Julian's uncharacteristically relaxed vocals, and seemingly sweet lyrics wouldn't be out of place at a 1950s beach resort for retirees. For the garage revival band of the 2000s, it is almost pretty. Then the chorus gave me the creeps, pulling the whole thing apart and putting together this story.

From lyrics about one half of a couple not understanding what the other needs and intonations of stalking, I crafted a metaphor for my experience with how terrifying Cognitive Behavioral Therapy (CBT) and exposure therapy was when my anxiety spiked agoraphobic tendencies. Our antagonist—who is also a somewhat sympathetic creature of nature—is applying the methods that they know to a mind that is not ready for them. CBT, while an amazing tool for many, was only a part of the puzzle for me. In terms of my recovery journey, it got me some of the way there, but **not all the way** (the second line of the song and title of the story). At times, it harmed more than it helped, but I was also complicit in that harm by convincing

myself withdrawing from the world was a safe and healthy
response to fear.

Summer (L)over

I recited shades of blue in my head: cerulean, azure, cornflower, indigo, steel, sapphire, powder, sky, byzantine… How can the clearest blue make me feel so disoriented? His eyes had me and they held me like a captive while his words licked a thousand wounds with his gentle, lilting accent. Usually, it would be impossible to be cool around such perfection, but he has the calming quality I've chased from a cliched combination of yoga, clonazepam, gossip doctors and designer shoes in the sale section. He's interested and interesting in perfect measure. He pulls truths from me with ease while endearing me with small, self-effacing statements and an adorably awkward hair flick. Physicists should study this man because he has some sort of effect on time. After all, this evening I'd dreaded and should have dragged was now liquid I drank up and could drown in.

I can hardly remember my behavior that night or how I managed to remain vaguely composed under the gaze of those piercing eyes, but my smiles seemed to please him and he gave affirming nods when I answered his questions. There was an easy flow between us, and I rode it. Our first moments were sensationally simple and reassuring, which perfectly tempered the instinct in me to kick it into overdrive and hurtle towards an all-too-familiar relationship wreckage.

Operating under his liquid time, we have to say goodbye too soon. I know I have to see him again. He casually enters his

number into my phone along with his name—a minor detail I
forgot to pick up in the haze of early-on-set obsession—Jacob.
Possessing the ten digits that could connect me to him at any
moment was like having the formula for happiness. In an
ordinarily ill-advised move, I texted him a smile emoji as I
walked away and held a party in my head when the heart symbol
appeared in return.

The brief textual exchange sustained me for the requisite
three days it takes for a guy to respond in this cruel dating
culture. He hits me with an adorable typo.

"I can see you."

Quickly, he amends it with a blushing emoji.

"Can I see you?"

It's a charming chink in his perfection, and I can see us telling
the story of him accidentally presenting as a stalker to our
friends and family in years to come. True lovers always need
these sweet little stories, and this is what I imagine being the
first of many. I agree to meet and let him make all the
arrangements, partly because I'm not sure I have any ideas to
impress him, but also because I want to see more of who he is
and what he wants. I want to be whatever that is.

I meet Jacob at a carnival and he tells me it's because it's
where his people are from. We laugh at his joke. He takes me to
the Tilt-A-Whirl, which would usually terrify me but by his side,
it is invigorating. I didn't even have to play the part of the girl he
wanted. He moulded me as he held me on our first gravity-
defying ride. He pulled the perfectly pitched performance of
terror and glee from me, letting him know that I was bold
enough for adventure but vulnerable enough to need his manly
support and that he handled me beautifully.

The pace of the night calms from there, and we find our—
his—pace with cotton candy and a delicious introduction to
butterfly chips. He remarks that it's refreshing to see a girl eat
junk food so I mentally schedule extra pilates time since I will be

an eater for him. He wins me a plush cat at the ring toss and is gentle with my utterly embarrassing performance at Skee-Ball. Then he leads us to the Ferris wheel. While we wait, I look up in anticipation and see stars. Not the dying ones light years away—those are washed out by the ambience of a thousand string lights on the ride that steer our fate. Those are our very own constellations.

On the ride, he tells me I'm beautiful and amazing. I am careful how I return the compliments, working hard to hold back the flurry of sentiments that threaten to fall out of lips that beg to be kissed. My lips get their wish soon enough, and our first kiss is at the highest point of the wheel's rotation. It's gentle yet intense. He lifts my chin with a delicate finger, raising my gaze to his before leaning in. His touch sends delicious chills down my core, which he mistakes for my being cold and offers me his jacket, slinging an arm over my shoulder as we descend back to Earth. Contact with him is electric. I imagine the lights on the ride flicker with our passion. They know us and how rare we are.

I take him home.

***

When I wake up, he's gone and yet still everywhere. His scent is on the sheets. I roll and writhe in them. His glass from our nightcap is on the counter; I lick the rim. The toy we won me is on the couch. I squeeze it until a seam rips. But most of all, he is still inside me. He's taken up space in my mind and body, and he's fucking welcome to it.

He says he's usually busy with work during the week, so I have to wait six whole days to see him again. The weather is pleasant, so he takes me on a picnic in the park. The spread is simple—a Greek salad, red pepper hummus, pita bites, a baguette with brie, strawberries, and a chilled bottle of Marlborough Sauvignon all atop a cozy blanket. There was nothing pretentious or too showy, and I adore that about him.

52

We get to know one another while we graze: we loathe the rise of populism in politics, lament at the state of journalism, worry for the future of climate change, and hope that the new A24 movie is everything we want it to be. We speak of his blossoming career in something vague and confusing. We agree on the importance of a strong skincare regime and find a shared nostalgia for bygone times when people danced in public together. He shyly confesses he's musical, and I say I want to hear him play. I hear of his glory university days and what all his mates are up to today. I could never grow tired of the subject of *him*. The more I learn, the more I'm dying to ask about former lovers. How many? Who? When? Why did they go their separate ways? I need to know so that we can avoid a similar fate.

With the questions burning in my heart, I'm relieved when a cheesy '80s ballad comes on from the playlist he's selected on his phone. We confess our mutual appreciation for it. He pumps up the volume and we sing along without shame, even though everyone is looking. Let them look. They might understand the momentous thing they are witnessing and wish they could share it, but they can't because it's ours alone. We're just giving them an envious peek at a connection unattainable to them.

We stroll back to my place, arm in arm. He strokes my hand, and I tease his immaculate hair whenever the fancy strikes me. Eventually, he protectively tweaks his locks back into place and says he doesn't like it, so I stop. I won't do it again. I stroke his hand, mirroring the pleasure he's giving me instead. He's quiet for a while, so I fill the silence with questions. They are simple ones—not the ones that have been plaguing me—but I want him to take up the air that my wrong move has sucked from the universe. I get him to talk about his family, or lack thereof, and I nod with deep care as he speaks of the importance of found family over blood relations. As I ache for him to go deeper so that I can find the wound in him and mend it, the discussion somehow turns to boundaries, and I know my misstep with the hair was more grievous than I'd thought.

Jacob says he has a specific 'hang-up.' For a moment, I hold hope this confessional is getting us somewhere good, but then he breaks it to me; his history means he has certain rules. The rules are about intimacy. They are numerous, but delivered with such sincerity that my heart hurts for him and the pain that must have forced these restrictions on him. Then he turns his blue eyes on me, takes my face between his hands, locks our eyes, and makes me swear I will not fall in love with him.

My heart no longer aches for him. The hurt transforms as his words stab me in the chest, over and over. A burning, strangling sensation rips through the left side of my chest, and I thrust my hand to my heart, trying to tend to the pressure. But he takes it for a vow on my behalf. It's no vow. I can't make any such promise when it's already too late. My body knows it and is screaming in pain. I keep all the agony and noise inside and say I understand. I try to convince myself it is just fear on his account, and for the first time, I'm a little afraid.

For *us*.

I'll do better—be cooler. More aloof, but supportive at the same time. I'll bend and contort into what he needs, starting with dropping my hand from his. The least I can do is give him that space. The other hand stays at my chest, a useless bandaid for the wound he's inflicted.

When we get to my apartment, I do everything he wants. I especially do not say *I love you* any of the thousands of times it runs through my head.

***

After the understanding is made, we meet almost every other night. Always at my place. He says he likes having me all to himself and that my place is so 'aesthetic.' I want to see his place badly. I try to imagine what it might look like, but I have no idea. He seems like he shares so much and yet he's still a total

enigma to me, but I forget all that when he's all kinds of
attentive. If I'm upset, he quells my fears; when I show
vulnerability, he tells me I'm stronger than I know; when I'm
aggrieved about the nothings of the rest of my life, he affirms my
feelings; and when he pleases me at night, he purrs words of
paise that send me into the abyss.

It's love. And that's when my heart starts to palpitate and my
stomach churns. I'm lovesick. I feel our easy, sublime
beginnings growing complications. My symptoms only progress
with his cummings and goings. Every night he leaves me with
the 'no love' reminder, and each time the heartache grows
worse. It's not emotional or metaphorical anymore. Now, when
he pleases me with his words or his body, it's physically painful.

Love is supposed to be the pain of someone's absence, but
with Jacob, it's mingled in with the pleasure of his company.
And it's not where I might expect it, not from penetration or
pressure from our more vigorous sessions. It was all in my chest.
With his head between my legs, all I feel is the veins in my heart
stretching. Not the kind I do at yoga, but a wrenching, tearing,
searing type of suffering. At the same time, I feel a puckering
tightness creating an arrhythmic beat in my whole body that
screams for the blood being starved from its core. The pain
burns so fucking bright it makes me buck and scream. Actions
he takes for orgasm. I don't tell him any different. I try not to tell
him much of anything. It feels like the only things that would
come out of my mouth would be gushing words of neediness,
screams of agony, or one of my organs.

One night, he brings over a guitar. He explains the many ways
it is unique and special, but all I hear is how he is special, and
that I must be too, because he is giving me this glimpse into his
soul. It makes me love him all the more. There's that saying of
something pulling at your heartstrings, but that's not quite right.
With every strum, I don't feel a romantic tugging in my chest.
What I feel is spastic misery and a stretching through my guts. I

know this guy is utterly transforming me, and even though it hurts, I don't want it to stop. I want him, and that means adjusting. At this point, he can shape me in any way he desires.

When he is not around, I still hurt. Constantly. When I take my increasingly strained breaths, it feels like an accordion playing. It's as if my verticals are not long and smooth, but bulbous from the infection of love. I am convinced the only way to end this torture is a declaration of love. It doesn't have to be the three magic words exactly—those can be so hard for men— but a display of deeper feelings. So I begin dropping hints of the millennial malaise and need to get out of town, if even for the weekend, and that he should join me. My hinting in the most extreme is greeted with a shrug and a mildly affirmative head tilt. The *why not* of body language. And with that, it was official. We were going on our first getaway together. The kind of trip that only lovers, or blossoming ones, take.

It was just post-season, and I get us a deal on a beachfront bungalow in East Hampton. Half the way there, he speaks of how much of a cliche we were heading to the city kids escape town. I counter with how much I wanted to try The Palm or Nick & Toni's, restaurants I had heard so much about. We'd never dined out together, just cozied up with takeout at my apartment. Jacob said we could travel the whole world of cuisine from my tiny place in Greenpoint, but I crave more; more places, more food all with him. It wasn't to be. He has us stop at a quaint Mom and Pop market to get supplies to barbecue the weekend away en route. He proclaims it romantic, and it is, because there are no two people better together than us, but it doesn't do anything to quell the swell and stretch in my chest.

Without unpacking, he demands a spontaneous swim. It's going to be chilly, but his desires are mine, and I change into my swimsuit. As I do, I catch a glimpse of my half-naked self in the mirror. Just above the line of my sweetheart bikini top is a burning red skin tag I've never seen before. It ruins me. I can't have Jacob see this blemish, so I throw on a cover-up to see me as far as the water, where I will immediately dive in despite the chill.

We tussle and tangle in the too-cool waters. It stings my skin and chills my bones, but it's a relief from everything else going on inside me. Jacob lifts me into his slight but strong arms with no trouble, as I straddle him and pull him tight to me so he cannot see my hideous new mark. He walks us out of the water in this manner, lowering us to the deck of our weekend home, and makes love to me. It is such a mix of pain and pleasure that I can't tell where one starts and the other begins. The usual orgasmic wave tears through me. But instead I of the rising and receding heatwave, there is a violent pulsation from my cervix to my chest, where it stays, threatening to combust. I scream. He seems to like it. I pull him toward me, partly to keep us connected, but mostly to press him to me, a pressure to keep in a mystery nightmare that might come out.

When the worst has faded and we've come apart, he tells me to shower while he prepares dinner. The cleansing of water running over me does not affect my wounds or worries as I see a new mole has risen while my heartbeat lowered. I can feel its lazy pace trying to strangle me from the inside. I collapse to the shower floor, trying to breathe. I may have passed out, but the next thing I remember is the reviving voice of Jacob calling me to dinner.

As the weekend continue, my symptoms grow. Here I was, having everything I wanted, and I was wasting it in pain and a disengaged demeanor. He calls me out on the latter, so I try to perk up. His blue, earnest eyes make it easy to transform a mood no matter what pain I am fighting, but a single tear traces down my face.

Jacob clasps my face, looking into me and says, "Don't do it."

I stop crying, but I don't think that is what he meant.

He walks out into the Atlantic, leaving me alone with my many horrid feelings. I swear, through blurry eyes, that his sculptured silhouette shifts. Like a glitch, his shadow self seems to blur and elongate on the vertical, for just a moment before he disappears into the deep.

He drives us home. He drives me home, at least. Stopping outside my Brooklyn walkup, he breaks the silence of the long journey.

"I don't think we should see each other anymore," he says.

My lips move and sounds may have come out, but they were incoherent at best.

"I told you about the love stuff," he continued, looking directly at my chest as though he can see how my heart was full and now fractured by him.

I hardly recall leaving the car. I disassociate directly to my home, where I stay until work calls to see why I haven't shown up. I must have been out of it for a full 24 hours. I beg off sick, and sick I am. This sickness isn't new but it's reached new levels of unimaginable. I'm debilitated.I slither my betraying body to the kitchenette, grasping at the cupboard handles to achingly pull myself up to my feet to get to the water my body screams for. And my body is actually screaming, I just have no idea what it is saying. It's some kind of hissing, slithering sound. Hydration is critical, though. Jacob always said so. He is so health conscious.

I try to gulp down essential fluids but begin to choke. The liquid goes down the wrong way and only inflames the writhing veins in my chest. My hand clutches my breast to pat out the choking feeling and soothe the churning inside me.

As I begin to level, my finger finds its way to that blemish. It has grown. Significantly. Now it is not so much a raised mole, but a nipple. Even that's not quite correct— it's odd, inverted somehow. Fingering it is a fresh pain, and I scream along with the terrible song of my insides.

***

58

I have not seen Jacob in two miserable weeks. With the help of friends who still tolerate the pathetic, post-breakup me, I removed his number from my phone and ruthlessly disciplined my social media activity. I go through the motions at work: present and absent all at once. It doesn't matter what company I am at, I might as well be in a hate machine. Anyone who isn't him enrages me, and that only aggravates the thing aching so harshly in my heart. If it weren't for the endless pain, I'd have thought I'd disappeared. And I am disappearing in weight.

People start asking me what diet I'm on, as though my ongoing affliction is aspirational somehow. I do not want to be losing pounds. I've worked hard for an ideal BMI and a perfectly fitting, carefully curated wardrobe. I don't want questions, compliments, food, or weight loss. I just want him. That is all. There is nothing else.

But that's not strictly true: there's pain even though there's barely a me.

***

The event had been added to my calendar. It was at the same place I had met Jacob all those months ago. A scheduled return to the scene of the crime that I can't avoid. I know he'll be there, and I will have to do a lot of work to hide the damage of his cruel summer.

I spend hours getting ready. I need to look perfect as a *fuck you* to him, but the agonies have taken their toll on me. More makeup than usual is required to cover up the dark circles under my eyes and lift and color my sunken cheeks. Dress selection is infuriating because my languishing, loving body is pointy in places there used to be the perfect hint of curve, and I need something that will cover up the skin tag that nags at my chest. All the while, I rehearse in my head the things I could say to Jacob that would cut him with casual cruelty or make him regret ever letting a good thing like me go.

When I get to the venue, I'm late and my colleague isn't outside to meet me like she said she would be, so I have to enter alone, hating her. The place is buzzing, but I'm so very alone—the loneliest girl in the world—and I'm being watched. The knots inside me tighten from pelvis to peritoneum. I can hardly breathe, and my gait stiffens against the pain. As I am about to crumple under the internal pressure, our eyes meet across the crowded room like they did on that first summer night.

He is speaking to another woman. It's like watching a warped movie reel of my own history. There's the casual way he couches her in his arm, penetrates her with his ocean eyes, flips his perfectly intentional unruly hair, and smiles only from one side of his mouth. I imagine them having the exact same conversation that baited and fated me. The whole thing is obscene, and I feel sick. I crumple over, barely managing to brace myself on the bar. In a flash, he is on me—Jacob. He takes me by the arm, guiding me away from the party to the dark side street of the restaurant.

He's back! He's here, and he's taking care of me, I think like a fool. I let myself sink into him and be guided by the strength of his embrace, but there is no comfort or care there. His grip on me is as tight as his pursed lips. He's pissed at me.

Now that we're alone, I vomit, and he pushes me against the wall, away from him and his precious designer clothing. It's all burning bile, and a strange fullness in my chest pushes at my breastbone with such force it threatens to explode. The contents of my stomach aren't the only thing I throw up. Now it's pain and accusations. The words of insecurity and pain flow until I blurt, "I love you!"

He looks disgusted and shrinks away from me as if those three words are the worst thing he's ever heard. As he retreats into shadow, he seems smaller, uglier somehow. Even though his perfect features are all intact, they morph in the shadows and throw shapes that don't make sense.

"I told you not to do that," he says, tossing his hair and disappearing back into the party.

I slide down the wall, scraping my worthless skin on the way down to the floor where I've just puked. My breath is ragged and the pressure in my chest finally breaks. There is a great and gross eruption from my trunk.

***

Mal lifts the white sheet from the body. He spots it immediately—the pink puckered hole on the left breast. He hollers to the pathologist, "Hey, we got ourselves another one."

"Another what?" the pathologist replies. Looking up from the corpse in front of him, its chest splayed open like butterfly wings, he walks over to his assistant's client and sighs. "Jeez! Every year at this time, it's the same. A poor girl ends up on our tables with an asshole for a heart."

Outro

Content warning: Body horror, toxic relationship

This song is inspired by a few songs from Taylor Swift's album, *Lover*. Most specifically, tracks two and three: *Cruel Summer* and, the titular, *Lover*. While it immediately appears to be an ode to the first long-time relationship of the singer, the lyrics of so many of the songs are filled with an anxiety unusual for the artist who has built a career on burning ex-lovers with confidence and good for her.

Indeed, opening our hearts to someone comes with a certain amount of anxiety. Those early days of love daze are when we are at our most vulnerable. But so many of the songs speak to an insecurity about their status as she hopes they can "always be this close," vows to always "save [him] a seat" as the man in question is notoriously private about their relationship and worries of how a separation would wreck her in *Cornelia Street*. There are also notes of *Blank Space* from *1989*, though stripped of all its self-awareness as this character "find[s] out what you want," and "be[comes] that girl for a month."

From personal experience and watching this singer live her loves in the spotlight and sing her soul about those experiences, I know hearts can be such assholes. This is literally that.

Growth Era

Her breast squeezed between two icy plates, Sara squinted her face and clenched every muscle in her body as the mammogram technician asked her to hold her breath. She wished she could escape the discomfort of the metal clamping down on her, but her breasts that had decided to swell and nipples that were slowly spreading had forced the situation a full decade before mandatory screening.

At last—after less than a minute—the mammography operator came and loosened the pressure of the slabs, imprisoning the body parts that were making themselves strangers to her. Before she could exhale the relief, the technician quickly maneuvered her into a new position and squashed from directions anew, but no better. The promise of "Just a few more images now, Sara," from the technician didn't help any. Not much does when you're nude from the waist up, freezing, and having sacks of fat contorted into pancakes because they are 'suspicious.' Quite amazing that this is our most sophisticated form of interrogation.

Dressed but no more dignified, Sara was told that her results would be sent to her physician within the next week. There was no meeting with her doctor. Instead, there was an automated call from the hospital to return in two days for an ultrasound.

She cancelled everything that conflicted with the surprise appointment and lay grimacing on a gurney for forty-five minutes while a silent woman jabbed a jellied camera device into every inch of her breasts. As far as Sara was concerned, they might as well be stabbing her with spikes, searing hot pokers or a cat-o'-nine-tails for all the tenderness of the process.

Somehow, this was worse than having her sensitive tissue smashed in mammography. Sara had never liked having her chest touched. It wasn't an erogenous zone that brought her any pleasure in the play of sex, a fact that multiple partners had failed to respect. She hadn't liked their presence or appearance long before they mutated on her. It wasn't dysphoric exactly. She just didn't trust them. They were like traumatic growths that made her eternally wear the reminder of death. These things had killed her mother, and now it looked like they were gunning for her. When they had been small, she could almost ignore them by quickly shoving them into a sports bra after necessary nudity and they didn't tug at the lines of her clothing, making themselves a nuisance to her clothed life.

Sneaking a glance at the screen, all she could see was a long series of images lined up in a way that reminded her of those old photo booth strips. Every image looked like the black void of space with slight interruptions of light or alien texture. But these lights in the dark had no beauty like the nebula she'd seen in documentaries or textbooks. Despite having no idea what she was looking at, the more she looked, the more the lines and lights contorted into monstrous forms. One morphed into the features of a scream, distorted in its torment and pleading with her for help that she couldn't offer. Another reconfigured into burning eyes with a toothy grin that she imagined mocking her as it devoured healthy cells and spat out chaos. The worst were the blank ones that she couldn't read. It was like looking at the art exhibit of her own body and the meaning escaped her. She searched the images uselessly and was relieved when the quiet

technician turned the screen away from her because she didn't
want to be at this art gallery anymore.

***

Things started to happen in quick succession: another
mammogram and ultrasound duet followed by a phone robot
impersonally inviting her in for a bilateral biopsy. After two
agonizing weeks, Sara found herself in front of a doctor for the
first time. While she was topless, he explained that they would
be extracting two 'suspicious' pieces of tissue but by different
methods because they were each only visible under different
scans. What they took away was to be replaced with 'clips,' little
pieces of metal that would forever mark the location of the
excised tissue. Placing these tiny markers would let them
identify regions that had been tested for the future.

This was when Sara learned that redheads have a high
tolerance for anesthetics. An anti-superpower that had her
howling in pain as she felt the chunks being chopped from her
insides and the minute fragment of metal being inserted into
flesh. For round two, they gave her a stronger dose of anesthetic,
but the experience pulled her under into a level of dissociation
so profound that they could have done it drug-free.

Before she knew it, she was back for biopsy number three and
more imaging. Then more imagining. Then at last a face-to-face
with her general practitioner who, while digging through the
extensive files of a woman of a certain age, declared that she
hadn't had a biopsy, let alone three. Not realizing that this
appointment would be conducted by gaslight, Sara was furious.
Should she show him the unhealed wounds? She's had her tits
out plenty already of late. What was one more show?

She was saved from the display as he eventually found the
files and described with incomprehensible clinical jargon her
situation: hyperplasia and carcinoma, all three masses, pre-
cancerous. *Triplets!* The 'pre' part didn't sound as pretty or

reassuring to Sara as it should have. For her, this was all just an inevitability. The melt of time had her rapidly approaching the age when her mother was diagnosed and it had been a long agonizing wait to confirm what she knew: she was born with bombs strapped to her.

"They are common," the doctor assured her. "You just don't really want them inside you—"

"Like men," Sara found herself saying. The jest cut no tension.

They just stared at one another for a moment before he described the need for surgery, the effects that this type of extraction might have on her cosmetically and how she should reach out to her insurance company about coverage while she waited for a surgical consult.

***

Sara left, feeling dead already. She was numb for some time, but hours later when her body and brain woke up while sat on the couch with an untouched glass of wine in her hand, distress engulfed her. Had she heard that she would be okay? She was not. Not okay at all. She wanted to scream; she wanted to know more but was afraid of what research might yield. She wanted to talk about it for hours, but she wanted to hide it from others so that she might hide from it herself. Her body was not right and there was nothing 'right' she could do about it. She disappeared her wine.

It was just her and the three toxic things growing inside her.

***

The next week, Sara met with the surgeon. She liked him, considering he was a guy who wanted to take a knife to her. He spoke plainly and checked in on her as he examined her breasts, a care that other healthcare practitioners had not extended to her. She thought it was going as well as she could have expected until he delivered the frustrating news, "Scheduling the surgery will actually be relatively quick, we are just having trouble locating one of the cysts in your right breast so we will need to do some enhanced scans."

One of her cysts, lumps, whatever, had gone missing. *Missing?* Was this a case for the medical police? They had been tagged and were under house arrest, after all. How could this be happening? There would be no answers to her questions. Time was up for this consultation in the strangled and overwhelmed healthcare system.

Then there was the waiting. There is so much waiting. Six months and the scan still hadn't been scheduled while this rogue thing was growing somewhere inside her. The wounds from her biopsies hadn't completely healed and she could feel the scar tissue forming, like a slow and subtle hardening along the path where the needles penetrated. If her movement caused her to jiggle, she felt something strange, and each time wondered if it was just her healing body or the missing mass making itself known to her.

Sara was starting to hate her breasts more with every day that passed with no answers. She had to do something, so started her own search party for the missing piece of potential poison hiding in her. She'd try anything. Science was moving too slow. She needed relief immediately and would try anything.

***

Sara started with a woman who worked with crystals, employing her for her scrying abilities. The jewel on a string swung over the bare chest Sara could hardly stand to look at anymore. It was searching for the tiny stray piece of metal in her, to no avail. As she paid for nothing, the holistic practitioner said that Sara had a lot of tension that she could help with. *No shit, I've got tension*, Sara thought, handing over a small fortune. *My body's trying to kill me, but not without tormenting me first. That would stress anyone out.*

Next, she took herself to a tarot reader. It wasn't Sara's first. She had a deck at home that she found helpful for working through the nonsense daily life threw at her, but she had a professional grade question this time. She needed to know if she was in danger and if this situation would resolve itself soon. She decided to put trust in the cards to care for her in ways that she felt doctors had failed to.

The simple three-card spread was laid out before her. The Hermit in its upright position, The Chariot reversed, and The Fool, also upside-down. She hears things from the reader that she already knows: she is looking for something and the answers are in her already. While technically accurate, the reading is maddening. She needed something with more depth and action-oriented.

After the underwhelming result from the scared deck, Sara tried a tasseographer. She drank the tea down and was faced with the shape of two round breasts. She commissioned a poppet from a mystic instructing them to place three small pieces of metal inside the truck of the doll. When she received it, she tore it open. Each tear was mirrored in her body, stabbing and searing pain coursing through her core but leaving no trace. She worked through the hurt because she was on a desperate hunt. Having shredded the doll to pieces, she could only find two of the three pieces of metal. The third eluded even her magical double.

Sara ventured to a palm reader with an unusual request, that she look at her breasts instead of her hands. She was refused. It was all quite embarrassing, but she trooped on with a fresh idea: consulting a spirit board. She did not have one, but that was no matter, she had everything she needed. She drew *yes, no, goodbye* and the alphabet across her chest in the rough formation of a board and used her finger as the planchette. Sara asked the spirits if they knew where her disappeared cyst was. She cleared her mind and let her fingers do the talking, drawing her index across her body she looked and it had landed on *no*.

The spirits were either not all-knowing, unhelpful, or right, and she was screwed.

Running out of ideas, she booked an appointment with an astrologer. She provided her birth date, time and location and when she arrived, the astrologist had made a complex chart. It was a map of the sky with lines criss-crossing and swirling around making connections that meant nothing to her but looked beautiful. Unfortunately, the answers she got were not beautiful, but predictable. She was told that with Venus in its current location, she would be having trouble with clarity and would not find the answers she sought without looking deep inside herself.

Sara went home feeling more depressed than ever. She poured herself a consolatory glass of wine, then another, and turned on the television to continue her rewatch of the X-Files. She was on season 3 and this episode was one of her favorites. A man could see the future but only other people's deaths. *I'd like to meet that guy*, she thought.

There might be some relief from knowing what line-of-sight death was in.

That's when one character uttered the word—anthropomancy. With the minor buzz and the advice of the astrologist running through her mind—*look deep inside yourself*—an idea took its terrible shape. She looked up anthropomancy on her phone. It was the practice of prognostication by way of reading freshly spilled entrails. Positively disgusting archaic stuff, but desperation had her mind working in unusual ways and devised a way she could adapt this craft for her own purposes. The answers were inside her. She just had to find them.

***

Sara collected the tools she needed; a drop cloth, utility knife, clean tea towels, painkillers, rubbing alcohol, and her tablet open to a page with a picture of breast anatomy displayed. The portrait of ordinary breasts sparks determination and rage in her. She's always had a fraught relationship with the exterior of her chest and now, with months of developing feelings, she hated and feared the interior even more. This figure, rendered by a doctor, was also a reminder that they couldn't help her. She was going to have to take care of it herself. With the hatred for her betraying breasts brimming, she didn't see what further harm she could do.

She laid the cloth neatly on her dining table and arranged her other equipment around her before stripping her top naked and resting her breasts on the surface. Dry swallowing the maximum recommended amount of the tablets to numb the pain, she applied a liberal amount of the antiseptic over the curvy top of each boob and picked up the knife. She held it up, its shine inciting the slightest amount of fear. Inhaling, Sara stared down at the sharp instrument until her tipsy self won over the fear with false confidence.

Starting with her right breast—the worst offender—she cut. Like that first biopsy, she felt everything, and it was torture, but sheer determination got her through the thick layer of skin. The pressure required was surprising and the soft, wobbly meat fought her all the way, creating an uneven score down the flap super to the nipple. Blood trickled out of the gash and onto the cloth beneath her. It was not quite as much as she might have imagined. Then she repeated the procedure on the left. She'd entered an ecstatic level of pain now with all the adrenaline coursing through her body. It made her hands shake a little when she needed them steady for the next stage.

Taking a calming chug directly from the bottle of wine, she carved hard lateral lines across the end of her first incision. She wanted to scream, but bit her lip and slammed her fist into the table instead. The bite was hard, and she tasted the tang of metallic blood mixing with the sharp citrus of the wine. *Just one more cut*, she told herself, and made another bloody slit over the other breast.

Breathing heavily, she took the final step, tugging her tits apart at their centers. Pink tissue and grayish fat spilled out before her. As gently as possible, she poked around with the point of the knife, looking for the metal markers that tagged her rotten meat.

There was much more fat to sift through on her left. She had been told surgery would remove all of this because it was a potentially dangerous excess from the hyperplasia. Sara began to carve at the grey and white spots she assumed to be the offending tissue and discarded the chunks onto the gory table with a squelch. Reaching a certain depth, she found the first clip just beneath her nipple.

One down. Two to go.

She began to dig through the viscera of her right breast where two metal markers should be. With less fat, there was much more blood, which she tried to dab away with her towels when the first marker appeared. It was nestled to the deep right in her flap lateral, according to the diagram. This one was more obviously an outsider on her insides, a pale hard and angular lump attached to healthier pink tissue.

That was two. Where was the illusive third?

She dove back in, this time with a precise plan: moving left to right, going layer by layer, but there was nothing. Not a single sign of the shiny metal marking the enemy within.

Sara was feeling woozy by now and her vision started to dance and she thought she saw the extracted fragments and marked masses dance too, mocking her with playful movement. Blinking hard, clarity of vision returned for a moment and there was nothing but the mess she had made. Nothing. Weakening again, thoughts and sight swimming, she found the truth in the nonsensical shapeshifting in her view. There was no sense and no meaning to what she was going through. No meaning in life, death, or breasts, but she'd never felt closer to or more comfortable with them now they were destroyed. *They're just things*, she thought, as she swooned and fell face-first into her own bloody deconstruction.

Outro

Content warnings: cancer, self-mutilation

This is a true story... to a point. As I'm writing this, I am waiting for one of the marked hyperplasia masses in my breast to be relocated. Relocated the fuck out of my body. I knew something was something wrong when one of my breasts changed significantly and I hid from it. I tried not to look at it. Never let it be touched by lovers who meant well. I changed bras a thousand times. I changed the way I dressed to deemphasize the growing size of my left side. It wasn't a surprise. I've been waiting for my breasts to betray me since I was old enough to understand what killed my mother. Luckily (?) with my family history I am scheduled for early and often breast screenings so they caught what I wanted to deny.

After an initial mammogram (super fun), things happened a lot and very quickly. Over six weeks, including the winter holidays, I had appointments for scans, consults and procedures at least twice a week. My surgeon made it clear that I do need surgery to remove a number of masses and general weirdness and that I do not have cancer *yet*. He said *YET*. Since all that urgent and, frankly, concerning activity, it's been over six months of waiting for a special scan, I need to find the missing cysts. I follow up every week trying to get things moving because the waiting isn't great for my anxiety and depressive disorders so that has meant a whole other set of appointments with therapists and psychiatrists to help me continue living a minimal amount of life under such uncertainty. Medication is helping, as is writing this in some fucked up way.

Unlike other stories in this collection, I knew it was something that I needed to write and it didn't originate in song, but it became what it is by musical influence. At one point, I was

so over all of it that I was tempted to book a plane ticket to
anywhere just to go through TSA because those guys would find
my missing metal for sure. That's when I realized the whole
situation was actually kind of funny and it was the humor and
exhaustion of *Body* by Mother Mother from their excellent 2008
album, *O My Heart,* that made this tale take a turn for the
absurd. The lyrics are genuinely comedic genius punctuated
with a genuine tiredness for "a cumbersome and heavy body."
The track perfectly describes my relationship to my body at this
moment because it is a ridiculous mess, to the point of hilarity
but so draining and demeaning at the same time.

Blind Thirst

Hank; Matthew; Jennie; Damon; Ben; Min; Carlos; Theo; Umar; Miles; Tara; Robbie; and Jacob. They all loved me. I hated it. There must be something wrong with them to love a creature like me. You just can't trust it. It must be some sort of certifiable deficiency.

I know, instantly, that Nick is different. He has the shaggy hair, tight jeans, and retro tee of an asshole. From across the bar, I get the vibe that he is in a band and has hidden tattoos with no meaning other than irresponsibility and stupidity. That he tries—and fails—to be vegan; works a scuzzy day job that he loves to complain about; drinks on the daily; never talks to his mother... and probably has barely tolerable hygiene.

I want him immediately.

I go get him.

I want a man. They are so much easier to hate and quicker to hate back.

Within a week, we are hot and heavy in all the ways that I want: equal parts sex and blazing rows. Both raise the hairs on my arms and send shocks of electricity through my core in the most delicious manner. They fill me up in the empty spots that you created.

He calls me stupid, just like you did.

He smashes things in rages, just as you would.

He combos swear words and insults as if he trained under you.

His love taps aren't as true as yours, but we're just getting started.

He can dismiss me just as well as you.

His hollering rivals yours.

He asks to borrow money almost as much as you.

His glares bore nearly as deep as yours could.

He plays the victim like he's bidding for an Oscar.

His gaslighting is getting better.

He overprotects and is suspicious at a professional level.

His guilt trips remind me of you.

He can coerce like a cult leader.

He's everything you taught me a man is. The only thing you ever taught me.

He's terrible.

He's perfect.

Everyone tells me I should leave him, but they don't understand the needs he feeds, needs bred into me. Needs that build with every feast of fury and neglect. When you used to treat me these ways, it hollowed me out. I was so sensitive to everything that I learned to become numb to the world. I spent years walking around as if a ghost, passing through life and experiences like vapor. I was nothing and no one, as you wanted me to be. Nick is waking me up with disrespect like devotion, fists like hugs, and contempt like a comfort blanket.

He screams that he hates me, and it satiates some strange hunger. The words fill me so completely. As the months go on, I feel the changes. I'm mean—vicious even. Not just to Nick but my friends and work colleagues. It's as though I want to provoke them to explode with and ire I can soak up to feel sated. The people closest to me start to pull away and he's changing, too. He seems drained. His bluster is losing its bite, less of the same hateful heart behind any of it.

I'm losing him, but not my craving for the hate he only half-heartedly hands out. I'm ravenous for it and will get it, whatever it takes.

"Hate me!" I scream.

"I do," he replies, limply.

"Hate me with passion and pain," I cry. "I'll eat it up like love."

"You're fucked up," he says.

"You were too," I reply. "That's who I need, that guy. I was a glut for your punishments. Punish me!"

He just walks out. His head hung, hair lost its luster, tight jeans now baggy. I know he's leaving for the last time because I've used him up, drank up all his hate and loved every drop of it. My appetite is whetted now, and I'll need fuel soon to sustain myself. I go out to hunt for a new Nick.

Outro

Content Warnings: References to physical and emotional abuse.

"I eat your hate like love," is a Bikini Kill lyric from *Feels Blind* that has always stuck with me. Not only does Kathleen Hanna's exceptional voice exude the rage of pain in the words, but I related to the experience of abuse and neglect the song speaks to. There is another line in the song that informs this story: "Look what you have taught me, your world has taught me nothing." I subvert this because when you learn to accept hate and hateful treatment, it can fill you with its poison. There can be something addictive about the hate that is hard to describe, but it is all-consuming, and I experienced this in a very intense relationship borne of trauma bonding. We lived in the hate that we had experienced, and it was deeply unhealthy. We were vampires, feeding on the trauma instead of processing it or professionally treating it.

I have happily, but with great difficulty, moved on now. I'm in a place that reminds me of how Hanna talks about moving on from the anger that fuelled Bikini Kill to the formation of Le Tigre in the documentary, *The Punk Singer*. I paraphrase, but the sentiment is that the rage is exhausting, and she was ready to start making music that celebrated everything she has instead of wallowing in the past and everything denied to her. I've had my Bikini Kill era, and it was a hell of a time. Now I'm most definitely in my Le Tigre era.

Cut You Like You Want Me To

I slide the door closed with as much force as possible, hoping it will come off the rails or at least approximate a slam. Like life, it disappoints me. I turn to give the door, and by extension the people behind it, the finger. This flimsy piece of rolling MDF is all I have to mark the beginning of the territory that's mine—in as much as anything is *mine*. I don't even have a real barrier between me and their bullshit.

My kingdom for an attic to go mad in!

I rip the poster of feckless female pop band faces off the back of my excuse for a door. It's been defaced, but somehow made it through the violent cull of my latest identity crisis. The crisis being that I desperately needed one and had been trying so many on that last year I was performing personal identity abortions on a monthly basis. The procedures were way too late for my father's liking, but fuck him. I'll be stubbornly alive if that pisses him off even a bit.

I've found myself now. Or did something find and perfectly form me? I dunno, but I knew everything I'd ever need to know about myself and the world the minute I listened to that cassette. Even with the background stank of a hundred previous recordings haunting its tape, it was fucking perfect. The grime only enhanced its raw and terrible beauty. I was born in the sludgy distortion of its licks and the anguish of its lyrics. I was awakened by its thunderous power chord riffs.

I've liked, even loved, music before. There's always been a soundtrack running, making meaning of the events of my stupid life, even if it was only in my head.

There was the first time I heard '50s sweetie-pie pop. That passed my eighth summer with romantic beauty vibes that don't exist anywhere near the shithole valley town where I live. Every time I rode my bike, it was like I was on the way to see some sweetheart. When I swilled 25p pops, in my head they were glass bottle colas or a milkshake served to me and my girls in a diner booth to share. I walked with a forced little *swish* in my hips, pretending that I was twirling my imaginary poodle skirt. It was all stupid, but it was my stupid. All mine.

I was barely a tween when I started listening to provocative princess pop. It felt so powerful to have girls singing to me. Especially about stuff I didn't quite understand, which made my parents uncomfortable. That's how I *knew* I was on to something sophisticated. It made me wonder what I would sing about. So I started collecting cutesy notebooks and filling them with vomit and calling it 'poetry.' Honestly, I'm amazed I could write anything down, what with being weighed down by the 5000 or so bangles on my arms and the wispy fringe (self-cut, thank you very much) eternally in my eyes.

Reminder to self: burn the journal evidence later.

Then I realized that the women I was listening to were just singing *at* me. These girls weren't singing for me. I wasn't interested in sexual power over men or turning girls envious (okay; I was a bit, but that's not the point.) I was deeper and darker than that, so I welcomed rock into what might be my soul; a.k.a. my off-brand stereo.

I discovered the most important band on Earth on the late-night pirate radio show, The Sessions, hosted by the legend Eddie Bolt. He left his old mainstream FM station because they wanted to censor him after he'd been bringing underground phonic fuckery to musically malnourished kids like me for decades. He was older than dirt, but still cool. My father even used to listen to him. With such a radical influence in his youth, you'd think he'd be more chill.

Bolt introduced the band with a brief hype… or maybe it was a warning. "You won't believe your ears, how they embody your fears." I was rapt. So possessed that I forgot the subtle art of simultaneously pressing 'play' and 'record.' I still don't have that song. I haven't heard it again. The only reason I'm sure I ever heard it in the first place was the call-ins on Bolt's next show. Kids from across the country were begging for a replay. But the tape was gone. Damaged. That didn't stop the masses from asking, though. After three sessions of being inundated with requests, Bolt played what remained of his recording just to prove to us that it was ruined beyond repair.

The sound was painful, literally. For a second, I knew what old people were talking about when they complained about modern music just being 'noise.' It was an audio atrocity. Acid being poured into my ear canal.

It's impossible to describe beyond the fact that it physically hurt. It only lasted seconds because its frequency blew out the broadcast signal. The air went dead and there was no more show that week.

One guy at school said he'd recorded it, but when he tried to play it back, it was just channel-scanning fuzz with little bursts of song, disk jockeys, and ads. He played it at break but, honestly, he could have just screwed up the recording or recorded air for attention.

I don't remember the real song fully. It's always just out of my grasp. I'll think I'm close to grabbing something of it and then it's just gone like vapor. Sometimes I catch myself humming a dark tune, but the second I'm aware, it disappears. Like, the other day, I was in Maths class and I was tapping my compass on the desk absentmindedly and everything in my head went silent. A silence so freaking absolute I felt like I was out of time and space, but I could see everyone else in the room tapping along with me.

I was frozen, apart from my tapping hand, and craving to know what this metallic orchestra was playing.... was it playing *the* song? But I was deaf to the sound. It felt as if we were making—remaking—the song in a weird kind of worship. No one blinked. We just soundlessly pounded our desks with our compasses in a ritual that I prayed would bring the actual sound back. But then, in a blink, I was back to a bland reality with dull sounds and the spiked end of a math instrument stuck in the flappy, pointless flesh between my thumb and index finger. Blood trickled out of me, but not much. It was like I'd hit the exact same spot with every blow. Freaked, I looked around the room. Only two other kids seemed to notice and they had matching marks on their fists. No one else seemed to see, so we kept the silence and did our stupid sums.

I still didn't have a handle on that first track, like a sonic specter haunting me. Occasionally it sends shivers down my spine when it walks over the graves of pains I thought I buried, but its resonance is reassuring. It's telling me, 'I understand.' It wakes up my rage and tells me it's okay to be mad or sad or whatever I need to be.

Then, a couple of months ago, Eddie Bolt announced that The Sessions would have the exclusive play of the band's first album. He was going to play one track a week for eight weeks. He hadn't even heard the whole thing himself because songs were being delivered to him weekly in time for the show.

It was all very mysterious and exciting and I sure as shit wasn't going to get caught out again. I record the whole show every week and am slowly splicing the album together from the full recordings using my twin deck. I've made a dozen copies of my mixtape version because that first track taught me how fragile and impermanent everything is. I'm not losing this musical lifeline again. I even make their j-cards with care instead of my usual scrawl.

I've listened to it about a million times and it's always whatever I need. It seems to be what anyone else who listens to it needs, too.

Track 2, *Pretty Pointless*, is pure angst. It's perfect for stewing in my rage against stupid controlling parents, unfair teachers, unbearable peers, and the garbage everything my little life has to throw at me. When I listen to it like this, I'm still and silently cry or let it do the screaming for me. Other times, I just let loose and bang around my room, much to the annoyance of my parents.

Track 3, *Eternal Sound*, is pure heartbreak. The beat pulsates with an arrhythmia. At first steady, then the fall comes with hyper and vacillating tempo, finally there's the break and the rhythm is too tight, intense and all disordered. It's like a sonic mirror of how it felt last year when I fell hard for Terri Shay and she called me queer before stopping speaking to me altogether. I threw up the first time I listened to it. I still play it on repeat because it lets me know someone else out there has been through it, and I imagine them as a burned kindred spirit. Seriously, they should have sent this song up on the starship Voyage. It would make the stars weep.

Track 4, *Gentle Knife*, has revenge energy for me. It's heavy, droning and repetitive in a way that reassures me everyone who hurts me will get what's coming to them. It seems to be the most divisive on The Record. Megan Yee seems to think it's all about the harm we do to ourselves. She's a cutter, so that makes sense. Then, AJ Carpenter swears it's a provocation to start a riot and will be like some anthem to the revolution. I don't know what is being revolutionized, but she's passionate about it.

Track 5, *Dumb Numb*, is musical melancholy. It's subtle with an ethereal quality even though it's all distortion with reverb and feedback and an undulating vocal that is like a long, uninterrupted wail. It's like a wave that envelops me in its sadness but is a sympathetic comfort blanket at the same time.

Track 6, *Wicked Hysteria*, seems to understand what it's like to be a girl. There's an ironic frenetic sickly sweetness to the vocals while the guitar thrashes and feedback cascades like the rollercoaster of girlhood. Laura Hanson is convinced that playing underneath the harsh layers are the real voices of agonized women in asylums. Sometimes, I think I hear them too, but that could just be my own internal screaming.

Track 7, *48-hour Hold*, is a glorious mess. It's so gritty, raw and abrasive. It's chaotic and fuzzy. It's like it doesn't know what it wants to be—which I can relate to—but is perfect in its dissonance.

***

Tonight's the final broadcast. The eighth song. Kids around school have been saying that it might be a repeat of that first lost track and I've been buzzing about it for days. I've been craving it. The first time it played, it bored so damn deep into my soul it passed straight through, leaving an exit hole. I need it again to fill me up and make me whole or I might go insane not knowing exactly what I heard for the rest of my life. But it's early and I've got time to kill. Time that is killing me, so I grab my Walkman, snap the headphones over my ears and crash down onto my unmade bed, swivelling to rest my feet on the wall and hang my head over the edge of the tiny twin bed. My world looks more authentic upside-down. And I wait.

***

I fell asleep. How the fuck could I have fallen asleep? My head is pounding from the position I was in and it's disorienting to sit up. I shake it off and look at my alarm clock. It's 10:57 p.m. Just three minutes until Eddie Bolt goes live. I leap up and turn the power dial on my player. It's already—always—tuned to the station. Some standard Brit Pop is playing, so I'm not too late, but I still need to hustle.

I've got my routine down pat and the tape is in the deck, my fingers poised to press play/record at the perfect moment when Eddie Bolt speaks, "Welcome Session listeners in bedrooms across Britain," he says. "I've got what you've been waiting for, the final track from The Record by the mysterious band with no name—" An electrifying tingle of excitement rolls through my body. I've never been more ready for anything in my life. "And in a twist as wild as this whole journey has been, this final track is a replay of that lost first song—" So the rumors were true. I was going to get my second chance at the tune that changed my life but threatened to ruin it by disappearing. "Get ready to hit record. Here it is, Cut You Like You Want Me To."

The song starts and I'm instantly transported back to that feeling from the first time. It's an expression of true rage that courses through me, possessing me to move along with it as it moves my emotions into dark anger.

***

The aggressive drums hit first. They set the fuming beat for the tune with intense and punishing thrashing. Symbols occasionally punctuating, they sing out like they are in pain. I pound my hands, trying to keep up with the wild and heavy beat.

***

Invisible fists thump at her mother's chest and head with an almighty force, pinning her to her grotty recliner and punching the cigarette from her mouth. The pain and confusion strikes her as hard as the blows. Her face swells and chest turns deep purple. Then a strike to the neck leaves her choking.

***

The lead guitar explodes into a relentless wailing, delighting in sporadic bouts of grim and grimy distortion. I furiously strum my air guitar with determined arms.

***

With every stroke of her imaginary guitar, ghostly claws tear at her father's torso. Blood gushes through his stained white vest. As he rips apart, he wails harder at the guitar.

***

The bass joins in, choppy and discordant, giving an extra gross texture to the track and the rage that I feel. Then the playing turns tight and uses intermittent palm-muting, adding a whole extra dimension to the sound. Anger is so layered. I pluck and slap along on my pretend instrument.

***

Her father's chest is now an open cavity. He feels tugging and smacking at his organs. The pressure snaps one rib at a time, rupturing his trachea, and digging through to his ugly heart, which is smacked repeatedly into a dangerous rhythm.

***

Now the fierce and unbridled wall of sound has me bouncing, head banging, and spinning chaotically. My anger is so active and the raucous energy of the music is bringing it to life like nothing I've ever felt before. It's cathartic.

***

The bodies of her parents thrash violently around the small living space. Like rag dolls, they fly and ricochet off walls and furniture, smashing and breaking their soft bodies.

***

When it's over, I'm exhilarated and exhausted. I quickly take a fresh tape and add it to The Record in its rightful first place. Now my playlist is complete and I listen all the way through. I let it all course through me, entering me in an almost intimate way. I am The Record and it is me.

It finishes, and I lay in ecstasy for a while until I notice how quiet the house is. It's too quiet. There's no one arguing, shouting at me to keep it down, or yelling for someone to fetch them another beer. I'm tempted to enjoy the silence, but there's an ominous edge to it so I brave the living room and setting off the parents.

As I enter, I see the pure carnage. My is mother is splayed out on the broken coffee table, a bruised and bloody mess. Father is slumped in the corner with his insides hanging out. There's gore and viscera everywhere. From the state of them, I'm sure they are dead and I don't know how to feel about that, but I do know I don't want to be here, so I tread carefully through the crime scene and exit the house.

Outside, I inhale the fresh air. Looking up and down the tint terrace, I see the other kids from the block all looking equally bemused.

Outro

Content warnings: Body horror, reference to abusive home life, reference to self-harm

This story is inspired by *Disarm* by The Smashing Pumpkins. Singer and lyricist, Billy Corgan, has alluded to this song being about his abusive father and contains stunning—in both the beautiful and shocking sense-lyrics "the killer in me is the killer in you" and "cut you like you want me to." I take the title and end results of this story from the latter, while the former is embodied in the mysterious and profound effect of the fictional band.

Music can, and should, resonate with us deeply as the Pumpkins's epic *Mellon Collie and the Infinite Sadness* did with me. I still perfectly recall getting the cassette from Woolworths and scurrying (in as much as any sad girl taking themselves way too seriously 'scurries') home so that I could play it. I reclined on my twin bed in the box room I had just appropriately painted dark blue and adorned with gold stars. And was still while I absorbed its beauty for the full 2-hour runtime. I felt the anger and sadness in my bones and then I listened to it again and again for the rest of my life. But that first listen is where the bedroom setting comes into the story. A room is such a vital place for a girl. It's the only space that is your own. It's a sanctuary where you can do your private girl things and be/become who you are on your own terms.

In my teen years, my bedroom was always filled with music. Much of it was embarrassing, while some of it was world-altering and remain in frequent rotation for me to this day. In the spirit of bedroom music, this is also something of an ode to the escapism our favorite bands offer us and in those days you'd turn the volume up to eleven to let your parents know your feelings. Rock and metal would usually just get me a stern knock on the door and a "turn it the fuck down" request. But, here's a pro-tip for leave-me-the-fuck-alone vibes, put on Jeff Buckley. No parent wants to deal with whatever has precipitated the playing of that melancholic crooner.

The DJ featured in this story is also inspired by a genuine hero: John Peel. He was a British radio DJ active from 1967 to 2004. He brought alternative music to generations and was largely responsible for introducing the nation to punk. What a total fucking icon.

Fluorescent Adolescent

It's a bright but windy summer day at Dunure Castle on the southeast coast of Scotland. Nestled on a cliff, it offers a gorgeous vista of the North Sea, a small sandy beach, green hills rolling out for miles, and the mysterious labyrinth. Composed of mossy, mushroom-laden stones and running in nonsensical circles, it was supposedly a site used for pagan rituals. Just to the left of this sacred spot, Lulu holds back Em's hair while she vomits up some combination of amphetamines and the 'shrooms they just picked. Heaving up bile, it occurs to Em that the only thing higher than her here are Lulu's vintage velvet purple platforms which she narrowly misses with the ejected contents of her stomach. Feeling empty and slightly better, she spins to sit and swill her foul mouth out with the contents of her water bottle. Looking around at the crowd of hundreds gathered, it also occurs to her that the castle might be the only thing older than them here. All around them teens and twenty-somethings are incandescent in their youth, laughing, hugging, and dancing without a care. The view is as envy-inducing as it is exhausting. Em already had her youthful fun and made the best mistakes, but she wouldn't go back to it for anything.

Everyone was there for a once-in-a-lifetime full solar eclipse party. Em and Lulu just happened to be a bit later on in that lifetime than most of the revellers. It was a silent disco affair, not like the rough-and-ready ones Em frequented in the 90s where the DJ ran sound from CDs out of a gutted-out ambulance through ancient subwoofers. The acoustics were for shit, but the drugs were new and good, filling the attendees with love and energy and emptying them of any care about the sound quality or the future. They were so in the moment.

This was a whole new world of rave culture. A slick setup totally at odds with the historic pastoral setting. Strips of LED lights lined a chrome stage where a guy with a computer bopped along silently as he served out a variety of jams pipped via Bluetooth into headsets.

Marcus ran over to them, looking excited until he saw the pile of vomit next to Em. "Eww," he crooned. "I guess old people can't hold their wizz," he said, shaking his head. "And I thought your generation invented raves." Their junior colleague, who persuaded them to attend, was dressed with even more flare than usual in an unbuttoned silver waistcoat, iridescent purple trousers, a rainbow feather boa crossing his neck and glo-bands wrapping high up his wrists. "Come on," he sighed, lifting Em, "get on the dance floor."

The threesome weaved through writhing bodies, filling the labyrinth to find a space. They put on their headphones and zipped through the channels until they found a track that vibed with them. Em passed through a medley of unfamiliar pop songs that were probably released within the last ten years, and repetitive EDM, and genres she didn't even recognize. She settled on a classic from her generation to ease her in. The three friends grooved in a chaotic mass to different beats, Em occasionally releasing the headset from her ears to enjoy the dissonance of the roaring music and the quiet thumping of feet with low-level whooping and chatter. As she danced, she started to feel two things. First, that familiar connection to the masses and the music that had the power to take the edge off of the anxiety she'd been feeling about putting herself out there amongst the youths. Second, was how her body didn't seem to want to move the way that it used to. She could still find the rhythm, but grinding to it was the literal grinding of knees and hips. Accommodating her body, she decided to reduce the strain with a sway and elaborate hand gestures. No one seemed to notice or care how she moved. Lulu also seemed to be feeling the exertion as she complained about her shoes pinching her feet as she shuffled along to whatever music filled her ears.

***

The time was coming, and the DJ announced a 2-minute countdown over their headsets. Everyone put on their solar-safe glasses in preparation. Marcus's hands were gesturing wildly in some ecstatic dance, Em assumed. Then he plucked one of the cups from her ear and instructed her to turn to a specific channel. He did the same with Lulu. As the moon moved into a crescent position, Em had some sort of French house music blaring in her ears. It had a synthy funk vibe to it with a great hook, and Em found her body responding to it.

Suddenly it seemed like the entire crowd was in sync, all stomping euphorically to the command of the beat under the uncommon celestial event, while underneath them, their motions were summoning something up.

The countdown continued, matching the rhythm perfectly as the bodies on the floor grooved with increasing frenzy. As the countdown hit 40 seconds, Em's headset went dead. She smacked it, but only succeeded in hitting herself in the head and not troubleshooting the problem at all. Lulu pulled off her headphones. "Did yours go dead?" Lulu asked.

"Yeah," Em agreed.

Marcus continued his gyrating, paying them no mind. Em and Lulu carefully maneuvered out of the crowd and up the hill to try to sort out the problem. Navigating was made more difficult as the sky darkened, with the moon at the sliver of a

92

wane over the sun. They apologetically bumped into partygoers who were so immersed in sound that they didn't even notice.

Marcus beckoned them back, yelling, "What the hell?! You're gonna miss the big moment." Then, rolling his eyes, he waded his way to them, removing his headset. "What's up?" he asked.

"Technical difficulties," Em said, holding up her silent headphones.

"Fucking typical," he sighed.

"It'll still look awesome," Lulu consoled. "There's great energy. We don't need the music."

But there was music. It was the basey, primal sound of hundreds of feet stamping in concert with some deeper resonance underscoring it. That's when Em noticed it and pulled her friends away further up the hill.

"Look at them!" She exclaimed. The party had taken on a different tone and hue. The dancers were in perfect unison, swaying their hands, kicking their legs and twirling as one. The mass began to exude a fluorescence. Em lowered her glasses to check that it wasn't some effect of the lenses. It was not. The dancing mass was otherworldly in its luminescence, and limbs left light traces where they had been the moment before, leaving tracing effects across the dance floor.

"Wicked!" Marcus declared.

"It's probably just the 'shrooms kicking in," Lulu said.

Em wasn't so sure. She'd spewed hers up before they had a chance to get into her system, and what were the odds of them all coming up at once with the exact same hallucination? Darkness engulfed them. The three cast their eyes up to the awesome fully eclipsed sun, creating a blackhole above them.

That's when the screaming started.

Mistaking it for hollers of jubilation, Marcus momentarily joined in with a celebratory whoop, but it died on his tongue as he saw what was happening.

The labyrinth had come to life. The underground network of fungi many had partaken in just hours ago was awakening with savage results. From their short distance away, Em saw someone erupt into a million minuscule spores that caught in the breeze, riding the air, and choking anyone unlucky enough to be breathing in the vicinity. People started coughing violently and collapsing.

In utter shock, Em watched as one girl who had inhaled the follicles transformed. Her skin turned spongy as fungal growths tore painfully through her dermis. The same thing was happening to the guy next to her. She held onto him, uselessly, for dear life. His skin sprouted mushroom caps all over. One burst out of his mouth, making Em think of her earlier explosion, and she shuddered.

As the mushrooms consumed them, the pair slowed, finally freezing into grotesque human-shaped fungi formations on the labyrinth floor. And yet, the horror of it all was beautiful, transformed by the fluorescent glow. It was a dissonance the brain couldn't handle.

The sounds were equally terrifying. People exploded with squelching pops, while those with their flesh being infested howled in an unimaginable pain that bore into Em's eardrums like knives.

More was happening that they didn't understand. People were sucked into the earth as they begged for help that would never come. The hidden expanse of fungus beneath their dancing feet pulled bodies asunder to join their mega organism.

Unseen by the trio, a stem slithered its way toward them, wrapping itself around Marcus's foot. It violently pulled him into the fray. The stem wove its way into his nose and ears and other orifices as he was dragged away. Em and Lulu screamed after him, but he was gone in seconds. Just before his body was sucked into the dirt to disappear forever and join a superorganism, two mushroom caps pushed out his eyeballs. Bulbous, squishy, unseeing, and grotesque replacements for his famous baby blues. The luminous multi-color traces of his journey into descent lasted longer than him.

They should have run, Em and Lulu, but they were stuck, entranced by two simultaneous and singular events. One from above and one from below. Now a fresh fluorescent hell unleashed itself before them. The trees that the network of mushrooms tended to activated. Branches extended their gnarly branches and twigs like claws, grabbing at the remaining running bodies, tearing them limb from limb. The gore was gorgeous and glowing with the blood reds spraying out in an electric ombre.

Light seeped back across the sky as the moon began to move past the sun. The mushrooms and natural cohort withdrew. The colors waned with it all, but Em and Lulu clung to one another, taking in the final scene. An oil-slick rainbow of unrecognizable evidence sprawled out before them. Guts were glitter, blood spatter was shimmering, and leftover limbs were lush with luster. The site was an incandescent atrocity.

They didn't move until the eclipse had completed its pass. Under the cold light of day, everything was altered. The landscape appeared ordinary, but the mushroom populous on the labyrinth of rocks that had been picked over by the partygoers was now refreshed. There was a look of health and vitality to the ancient structure where moments ago there had been the mess of a massacre.

The only two remaining, Em and Lulu, took the short stroll to the beach, giving the recent dance floor a wide berth. They planted themselves in the sand, icy waves threatening to lap at their toes, and understood what deathly silence was. "What the fuck just happened?" Lulu asked after many stabilizing breaths.

"I dunno," Em responded. "But why didn't it happen to us?" she wondered, the phosphorescent violence played back in her mind giving her an idea. "You didn't do the 'shrooms, did you?"

Lulu nodded, "Yeah, I did. I was kinda hoping this is still part of the trip."

Em shook her head. "So it wasn't some revenge of nature going after the people who foraged from a sacred space."

"Do you know how bonkers that sounds?" Lulu replied.

"Was there anything not bonkers about what we just saw?" Em said.

"True," said Lulu.

Why would they be the only survivors? What made them so special? Questions ran through Em's mind as Lulu took off her shoes and rubbed at her feet. "At least they didn't get these babies," she said, waving her shoes. "They're vintage."

That was it. It wasn't what made them special, but *different*. They were the only ones over 40 there. The life of nature needed iridescent youth. They were old women and invisible to it. Em lay with that thought, knowing she'd rejoin nature soon enough, anyway.

Outro

This story uses the title of the song that inspires it, *Fluorescent Adolescent* by the Arctic Monkeys. It reminisces for wild bygone days of exciting and sexual youth. I flip this script, focusing instead on the fraught feelings of aging as a woman, or femme-presenting person. I'm not really nostalgic for the specifically sexual youthful antics that the song describes so chose to give voice to the older version of the woman represented.

For sure, youth has a brightness to it that we can't rekindle, but there is something I've enjoyed about aging in a femme body: increasing invisibility. I don't (and never will) miss the catcalls, street harassment, and requests to smile from strangers, that I received on a daily basis when I was younger. It was so taxing and demeaning and I thought it would never end. But it's reaching a clear conclusion. Here, instead of thinking back on sexploitations, I'm marking the quiet and appreciated disappearance from the attentions of men which we deem so natural.

Is It A Video?

Zoe stretched her eyes painfully wide, as if that could startle them back to life. The dregs of coffee number four—black, three sugars—sat in her designated office mug beside her. She was hitting her wall, the one that only the glow from her screen and monotonous inching back and forth between frames could run her into.

Stretching her neck in a full rotation, she checked the clock: still two hours left of her shift. It was time to switch over to her little side project. It wasn't *technically* slacking and besides, it gave her a minor bump to make it through the rest of the day.

She ejected the bulky Beta Max of a foreign dignitary, placing it reverently back in the correctly labelled case, then grabbed the extra tape she'd pulled that morning. It wasn't on her list, but she always took a spare from her collection of favorites.

Today, she'd taken Gideon's. His video had been on heavy rotation recently. Zoe was particularly drawn to him and his tape since the release of his latest film, a heartbreaking romance in which he gave a stirring and complex performance as man struggling with his sexual identity. It was critically lauded and the award nominations rolled in, cementing him as a Hollywood darling. She'd collected his entire movie back catalog on Blu-Ray at home and found herself watching and re-watching them. With a job that had her sitting in front of a screen all day, she usually preferred to spend her off hours immersed in a book or craft. Gideon was an exception. She had copious notes from all her viewings praising his acting choices and detailing how they made her feel. Such devoted and exhaling chronicling seemed like the least he deserved.

She slid his eulogy cassette into the playback deck of her tiny editing bay. As the tape played, she raised a finger to the screen, stroking his magnificent face.

And this time, the glow from the screen warmed her back to life.

***

Zoe was the memorial video editor at a TV station that broadcast nationally. She updated obituary videos for celebrities and notable people so they were ready to hit the screens the moment the worst happened. She was a one-woman department, and every day she went into what was referred to as the 'death cupboard' to fill her trolley with tapes and wheel them to her tiny editing room.

Her workspace was nestled in the broadcasting studio, so videos could be retrieved as quickly as possible in an emergency. She walked through the bustling workspace every day, head cast down, never speaking to anyone. They were all busy with their own lives and the stress of live broadcasts while she was busy with preparing the dead. They didn't really have anything in common.

She'd heard whispers of, "There goes mortuary Zoe," from time to time and felt the air chill before the coffee room emptied when she entered it one of her four times a day. Maybe they were a superstitious bunch who thought she carried the specter of death with her, but Zoe took her work seriously. She was a guardian of sorts and as the person responsible for preserving the memory of people who were beloved, she did her work with care.

The lives she memorialized were still being lived, always growing, with new achievements to be marked on the occasion of their death. She researched for news updates, reviewed current tapes for errors and erosion in quality, pulled new clips, and made the necessary updates.

She'd come up with her own rules for presenting the dead to the world. It was a carefully curated montage, beginning with a still image of them in their prime, preferably engaged in an activity related to the nature of their fame. The healthy stillness was then followed by them in action at various points in their lives on a four-beat. She found that this steadiness worked best, allowing for each image to be absorbed by the eye, reminding people of moments they experienced vicariously through the media of this person's life. The variety also suggested a celebration of life and primed the viewer for the emotional turn her cuts were about to take. After around twenty seconds of assorted images—giving the newscaster time to relay information on the individual—she'd move to a slow-motion shot of one of their most notorious moments giving the audience time to really take in the gravity of the loss before cross-fading to a more recent still image of them to cement a sense of pathos. Gideon's tape was a masterpiece.

Just because Zoe had a method did not mean that it was an easy job. There were 7326 tapes in the 'death cupboard' with more added all the time for the birth of a monarch, the election of a new governmental leader, or the rise of an artist (film, music, painter, etc). She could average seven tapes a day, meaning it would take her nearly three years to go through the full rotation of edits.

She had no plans to leave the job, so death was her life. She even listened to the radio news on the way to work to hear if there were any ailing celebrities so that she might prioritize their video. This was never something she was asked to do. In fact, she had no supervision and didn't need it. She knew her role, and she thought it was an important thing that she did.

Even if it was an invisible thing. It wasn't just the sheer volume of videos that made it hard sometimes, though. Part of her method involved treating everyone equally, so she had to put aside her feelings about prick politicians and the like to edit them with the same reverence as everyone else. Those days were trying, but she'd come away from them congratulating herself on her discipline and morals.

***

Morning reports hadn't declared any major ailments or tragedies for the people in her cupboard, so she was on her usual schedule. Her usual schedule plus Gideon. Zoe packed her cart with an ambitious ten tapes today and rolled them to her editing station.

She still worked on Beta Max because terminal budget cuts didn't allow her an assistant to digitize the footage, and she didn't have time with her schedule because death waited for no one. This also meant she worked with other relics of technology. Her desk had a GCS-50 editing control board, chunky dual tape decks (one for master edits and one for recording), and four CRT screens (she only needed two, but there was always at least one on the fritz).

If any of the station crew ever had to come into her editing bay, they scoffed at the setup. They were digital fiends. They didn't appreciate the patience and artistry of working with the constraints that she had. Besides, she loved it. There was a tactility to her work that was lost with the use of a mouse and modern software. She loved the feel of the dial in her deft hands, slowly toggling between frames to capture the perfect moment. A moment where there was no motion blur, background noise, body blocking, or unflattering facial contortions. The uniqueness of her skills and situation just affirmed the import of her work.

She was searching for her final updated image for an aging musician when the radio that kept her company all day announced something horrific: Gideon—her Gideon—was being accused of sexual misconduct and other abuses. Details were still scant, but the newsreader said the actor was now in hiding. Zoe couldn't believe what she was hearing. She gently fingered the tape of his she had smuggled in, passing her index finger over his name again and again in disbelief. It couldn't be true. She had pages of evidence of his perfection in her journals. How could he do such things?

In an unusual move, she left her station. The broadcast room was abuzz with newsies running around in a rush that was usually only warranted for the recently worthy deceased, terrorism, and natural disasters. Listening intently while the never-had coffee number five brewed, Zoe heard more details these professionals were privy to but couldn't report in accordance with journalist standards. From the whispers, Zoe gathered that things were much worse than she could have imagined.

Vile details spilled from her colleagues' mouths. Gideon was being painted a monster.

She scurried back to her room to watch his video for the hundredth time and try to reconcile what she was hearing with what she'd seen. She reviewed it over and over until her shift's end. It wasn't until she was on the way home that the realization set in. What she was seeing was something she had invented. She'd meticulously created this imaginary version of a terrible man with her method.

Was it the man or was it the method? He must be a better performer than even she had given him credit for. All she could see in him was lies. All she felt was the stab of true betrayal.

Zoe wrestled with it all at night, even in her dreams. Her sleeping mind was filled with vivid images of the degrading and depraved things Gideon had done to other women. She'd always only known him through images, and his harm intruding on her nightmares made everything all too real and clear. Zoe felt the sting of all his wrongs as though it had happened directly to her.

Hadn't he hurt her in his own way, after all? She'd tended to his soul as captured in thousands of images and stitched them together to display the perfection he faked. His lies made her a liar. It made her work a lie.

She knew nothing ever really happened to guys like him. Not over a trifling scandal of abused women, no matter how many stormed behind yelling, "Me Too!"

There was a rage in her like she'd never felt before, screaming inside and prickling her skin. In her ire came an idea. There was a small way she could hit back. Through her work. She'd just have to modify her method.

***

In her shock, Zoe had forgotten to return her tapes to the death cupboard as usual, so Gideon's tape was still in the deck when she sat down first thing in the morning. She turned on her radio to keep up-to-date on the story and got to work.

She pulled everything from yesterday's news: pictures of Gideon dodging the press, looks of terror on his once beautiful face as he left his Hollywood home in an SUV with blackout windows, implicating images from his own social media, along with a selection of clips from movies where he played bad guys and publicity shots where he looked his most smug.

There was no new news coming in on the Gideon situation, and it infuriated her. Surely, there was nothing else worth talking about on a day like today. Why was there no follow-up on this critical story? Sure, she wasn't exactly doing her job, but why weren't her colleagues out in the newsroom, just a few hundred yards away doing theirs?

Now she had what she needed to cut him up into the monster he truly was, but old habits die hard, and she struggled to get away from her method. It was nearing three o'clock and there wasn't time to take another full edit pass. But there was something she could try. She had the tricks of the editing suite at her fingertips.

Zoe pulled a blank tape from the shelves of her tiny office. Plying it from its packaging, she took the spork she'd used for her lunch and dragged it along the film strip, twirling the spools with her fingers to slowly forward the tape. She imagined she was piercing his skin instead of film. Now she spooled the reel in rewind, but not to be kind. She pinched the gentle film with her fingers at irregular intervals. The crunching sound of the procedure was satisfying as she imagined she was crushing his eyes and testicles.

Then she placed Gideon's original video in the player deck and the manipulated tape in the master recorder, transferring the images onto the corrupted one. She played it back, and he was now grainy and mildly malformed. She relabelled this bastardized version for the archives and slipped the original into her bag before leaving for the day.

***

Zoe was proud of her work on the Gideon tape, but it had put her behind schedule, and who knew how long anyone had left? Her future dead couldn't wait, so she got up extra early and headed to the office.

Listening to her radio, she caught the news headlines as she pulled into her parking space: the renowned and now-shamed actor, Gideon Spade, had not been seen.

Turning up the volume, she listened intently. It wasn't that he hadn't been seen precisely, but that he *couldn't* be seen. Not properly.

Reports said that he appeared faded and worn, a little fuzzy around the edges, somehow flattened to the world and covered in scratches.

Zoe was stunned. Was this her handy work? She scrambled through her purse, looking for her phone, and ran a search for Gideon. She needed to see things for herself.

There he was, looking like the degraded and scratched-up piece of shit she'd made him on tape yesterday. It was an impossible thing, and yet, it was happening before her very eyes. In the footage, Gideon looked clearly distressed.

Good!. How do you think you made all those women feel? She smiled. She was going to test the theory that she'd edited the real Gideon.

***

She fetched Gideon's video from the death cupboard, but today, she filled the rest of her cart with random tapes from the general archives. There was one very obvious way to tell if she was controlling the image of Gideon. She was going to use superimposition and splice him with random frames.

An hour later, just as the rest of the crew were rolling in to start their day, his already sabotaged tape had superimposed a bare ass to his smug face and inserted single frames of animated characters at various points in the reel.

Zoe returned the tape back to where it belonged and collected a random set of tapes for her cart. It was just to keep up appearances. She had no intention of editing today. She was going to be glued to the news that her colleagues were producing. She tuned one of her spare screens to the channel with anticipation. She didn't have to wait long. Gideon's face was pixelated, the way they blur out copyrighted and offensive material on television, but the anchor confirmed that the actor's face had been altered to the appearance of another part of the anatomy. *Now everyone can truly see him for the asshole he is,* Zoe thought. But there was more.

As the beat reporter followed the deformed Gideon running to his vehicle, the actor let out a bone-curdling scream as his form flickered momentarily. She'd only spliced single frames into his video so the effect was barely perceptible, but her keen eye caught his body contort into a cartoon and back again. Now she

105

was certain that she had her grip on him. In the tiny room she'd
spent years hiding away from the world in, she suddenly felt
powerful. She'd caused pain. Now she had a talent and a taste
for it.

***

Zoe's ordinary job seemed pointless and constraining now. She
was going to test the limits of her rudimentary technology. She
started stretching frames, which tore at Gideon's fleshy body.
Then she added her channel's branded captioning in the lower
third with text such as, "Gideon Spade: suffers spontaneous
penis shrinking" and "Breaking: Gideon quarantine of Ebola."
The words floated in front of him everywhere he went in the real
world. Squeeze zooms were next. Usually used for creating
effects in title sequences such as flipping the text or having it
bounce around the frame, it had chaotic effects on the body,
resulting in his figure randomly springing and stretching around
the world.

With every new effect she inflicted on him, his pain brought
her delight. How quickly she went from fan to tormenter, and
she could do it all safely from her editing bay.

The longer it went on, the more her conviction grew that he
deserved every wretched thing she threw at him. She was editing
him to justice. At least, she was for a while.

People were becoming fascinated with the inexplicable
Gideon phenomena, so much so that his cancelling was
forgotten and instead the public began to show compassion and
concern for the monster. Zoe was incensed, but she knew how to
handle this armed with the GCS-50.

The perfect opportunity came the next day. Gideon was going
to be a guest on one of her station's chat shows. The monster
that she had worked hard to render visible was going to be in her
building. It made her sick, but she turned one of her monitors to
the channel to find him sitting, a total mess of her

manipulations, on a couch with a sympathetic-looking host behind a desk across from him. It was time.

Cracking her neck and stretching out her fingers, the powerful appendages that were about to do their dirtiest work yet, she constructed a split screen. Smashing the save button, she looked up to the live broadcast and watched as Gideon suddenly stopped speaking. A thin line of red spread across his torso, bleeding through his white button-up and his top half slid to the floor. The cut was clean, but the bisection displayed his grotesquely juicy interior.

Chaos erupted in the studio and the screen changed to the SMPTE color bars, stating "technical difficulties." Zoe clicked the TV off.

While her colleagues rushed around in panic and paramedics arrived, Zoe cooly left her station, taking the original Gideon tape with her and dropping it on the news desk. They'd have need of it. Then she headed for her death cupboard. She carefully perused the shelves, plucking tapes with names of the egregious and unworthy.

Outro

Content warnings: Body horror, reference to abuse of women.

This story is an ode to the 3-minute single take of Timothée Chalamet going through the million emotions of heartbreak at the end of the film *Call Me By Your Name,* which is immaculately scored with Sufjan Stevens's *Visions of Gideon.* The lyric "Is it a video?" repeats numerous times. Instead of mining the song for meaning, this is a direct reaction to the sullying of such a beautiful film by the male co-lead, who turned out to be a real-life monster.

I address his villainy through my experience in broadcasting, or more specifically, my roommate's. She worked as a Continuity Announcer at one of the biggest networks in the UK. These cool kids keep your shows on the air and then hit the mic to tell you what is coming up next. In their offices, there really was a 'death cupboard' so that they could interrupt a broadcast at any moment if someone 'important' died.

I combined these two factors with my editing experience from an unused film degree by thinking about how we literally 'cut' footage. That has such a violent connotation, and I followed that through, bleeding the wounds into a strange fiction.

Stars & Scars

I'm not much of an artist, but I have one canvas I created something striking on. At first, whenever I looked at it, I felt hopeless and dejected. It was impossible to make this thing meaningful or beautiful.

After some time, it occurred to me: maybe that's not my style. Maybe what was inside me itching and screaming to get out was something ugly. I embraced it. Progress was slow at first, then I was like a woman possessed, and everything flowed out of me with incessant fervor.

The first person to notice my little art project was Jan at work.

"Oh," she said, pointing to the star on my long-healed wrist, "is that new?"

I nodded.

"Didn't take you for the tattoo type," she said. "What does it mean?"

I shrugged, and she turned away.

Everyone always turns away.

At home, David didn't seem to notice or care. Well, that's not entirely accurate. He cared when I did or didn't do something that inconvenienced him, and he let me know about it. Every time he did, I got a new star.

The first time was either an accident or necessity. I'm not sure. It hurt, but the kind of art I'm making always does and not because of the needles penetrating at my flesh. It's a deep pain, excavated and brought to the surface, oozing out of me with a few drops of blood. Then come the tears of sweet release.

I purge the hurts he inflicts and replace them with my own shapes, refusing his branding of me. The more rebellious the engravings I carve into myself, the greater the sense of relief each time I look at one of the permanent marks I've made. I am making myself a dark and exquisite piece of art wherever he tries to undo me.

As I fill my canvas, I become more visible to the world. My boss brings me into the office for an awkward conversation about dress code and 'respectability of appearance,' or some such shit, which completely misses the point. I'm invisible anymore, but he still can't see me. I think he wanted me to wear cardigans or turtlenecks to cover up.

I bought tank tops and shorts instead because soon I'd be ready for my exhibition.

I've lost count of the stars in my personal little galaxy, but there are many, and they all orbit me, making me into a sun that will blind them soon enough.

There's the cluster on my collarbones creeping up my neck like David's little 'love bites.' I've given myself an undercut to make space for my cosmic collection to grow over his backhanders. The back of my knees host two of my largest stars because they needed to cover the bruises from the kicks he gifts when I dare walk by. My toes bear the tiny twinkling remnants of where he stands on me to shut me up. Both shins and calves have quite the celestial mass of the different colors, shapes and sizes matching his slaps, pinches and jabs. I've got a starry selection on my belly where he doesn't want me to ever hold anything else. My thighs—his favorite place—now have concentric stars. Unless he finds a new secret spot to lay his hands, I may be looking at a supernova situation in this delicate region.

But my face is clear. The clever, stupid man never goes there.

I feel full, swelling with light and potential when I've always been meek and dim. That's how I know it's time. There's just one last star to create.

Late that night, I cut it into life on my left breast to mark a scar that even I can't see because he'd built up the internal bleed so gradually.

Now I was done, on multiple levels.

The next morning, I take my stars out into the light of day. In shorts and a tank with hair high in a ponytail, they shine. I am an illustrated woman, illustrating all the things that had been done to me for no one to see. I am a living, breathing constellation of the pain that had been carefully hidden. People are disgusted. They are disgusted with me. They still can't see through to the *he* who has done things to me.

I see how the world will end.

Outro

Content warnings: Self-harm, toxic relationship, emotional and physical abuse.

This is inspired by Taylor Swift's *Cardigan* from the *Folklore* record in which she refers to drawing stars around scars that make them bloody. This lyric is so vivid. Beautiful and sad. Before these words became the source of this story, they penetrated me, in that they encouraged me to get my first tattoo: my mother's star sign on my left breast and spreading to my shoulder. I wanted to keep my deceased mother close to my heart in a tangible, indelible way, but the location was right for another reason. It was an act of painting pretty stars around the scar of heartbreak that can never be mended.

When it comes to the stars of this story, they are a subtle nod to a cutting habit I developed in my teens. The reason I harmed myself was because someone was harming me, and it felt like a way of controlling the pain of life. I had an abuser. His speciality was psychological torment, but he was also physical and knew exactly where to strike so that no one would see the black and blue evidence that blossomed in its place.

I reported my abuser once to a school official. They did nothing, so I did not feel believed. My friends were aware that something was going on, but not the levels or the effect it was having on me. I was screaming on the inside and I just wanted someone to see and believe and maybe save me. That never happened, and it doesn't happen here either.

Summer & Autumn

Autumn

My sister is possessed. There's a demon living in her, eroding her soul and turning her into a monster. My sister, the monster. She's more than just a sister; she's my twin.

"Mom!" she shrieks. "She put fucking sand in my sneakers again."

"It's called penance," I say, watching her dump the grains out onto the mudroom floor, her eyes narrowing into a wicked glare. Because she won't repent, I'll have to take the lickings for her, so I pick up the pieces and put them in my shoes. They'll crunch and pinch when I walk all day long as her repentant by proxy. I don't know if it'll work but I am her double, and perhaps that stands for something. I'd like to be mad at her for everything— her behavior and making me do all her penance—but I work hard to practice the virtue of temperance.

"Why are you such a damn freak?" she hisses.

"Summer," Mom yells from the kitchen, "stop swearing. Autumn, knock it off. This is all getting ridiculous, and you're going to be late for school. I won't sign another tardy slip, you hear?!"

I say yes. She rolls her eyes and pulls a face at me. It's a grimace that makes the beast inside her visible.

Summer

I don't know what the hell is going on with my sister, but about three months ago, she decided to become un-fucking-believably weird. She got super into Jesus. Sure, fine, whatever. She gave away a bunch of her stuff—even some of mine—because she didn't want to live a material life. She started getting super judgy as well, telling me that whatever I did was bad and wrong in the eyes of God. She whispers preachy psalms to me like a super creep. Like, the other day, I was minding my own business throwing down breakfast because I'm eternally late for school—not wanting to go might have something to do with it—when she waltzed past, bumping into me saying, "The Lord will send on you curses, confusion and rebuke in everything you put your hand to, until you are destroyed and come to sudden ruin because of the evil you have done in forsaking him. Deuteronomy 28:20-22." What the fuck is that about?!

She also keeps putting sand everywhere. In my bed and my shoes, mostly. I have no idea where she is getting it from because we couldn't live further from the beach if we tried. It's all freaking me out, and Mom doesn't seem to notice or care. In fact, I'm the one who seems to be taking all the parental shit.

Autumn

At the front of the bus, while she horses around in the back with her burnout 'friends,' I scribble out the signs of Summer's possession in my notebook. Making the list might tell me just what I'm dealing with.

1. Playing rock music.

She got a guitar secondhand and strums furiously at it day and night, crooning angry, vulgar, and melancholic lyrics to her infernal songs. When she's not playing music, she's listening to that satanic metal noise that only heathens enjoy, and politicians are arguing over in court. She has hundreds of tapes and CDs of the sacrilegious stuff strewn around her abominably messy bedroom.

2. Got a pet snake.

This year, for our birthday, she got a python. She begged for the beast until Mom got sick of hearing about it and gave in. Serpents are creatures of the Devil. Deceivers that lead people into sin. She even named it Adam. This could be the creature that corrupted her.

For our birthday, I got the beautiful new shoes that are currently being ruined by her sinful selfishness.

3. Cursing.

Her language is appalling and heretical. I know she's smart and has a strong vocabulary because she used to get A's in English and wrote the most beautiful poetry. Now she writes obscene songs and every other word out of her mouth is a cuss. Everything is 'eff this' and 'eff that.' She knows them all and even combines them in nonsensical profane strings just to amuse herself and offend me. She even swears at Mom which is so disrespectful. This must be her demon speaking through her.

4. Doing things and denying them.

A few months ago, she started sneaking out at night. She comes home dirty and stinking of beer and smoke. If I catch her crawling back in her window at 2 a.m., she turns dark and threatens me with violence. The way she sneers her intimidations doesn't even sound like her voice, and her eyes are always wide and black. Then there are the smaller things: stealing from my savings jar; using my razors until they're blunt; taking my clothes without asking and ruining them with holes, pins, dye, or graffiti. When Mom confronts her about her behavior she casually and convincingly refutes everything. It's as if her possessor is making her forget all her sinful actions. This might mean that they are not totally fused yet and there's time to save her soul.

5. Sex?

I think she's been fooling around with guys and maybe girls. It's not like I care who she crushes on, but we had a pact to save it for marriage, and I don't know how far she's gone. Heck, she's even making out with Grady Maddox on the bus right now for everyone to see. It's a sickening display.

6. Change in appearance.

She's started to look different. We're barely identical anymore. She's been stricken by acne and cakes on dark make-up to cover it all up. The impurity of the soul is manifesting in her flesh. Not to mention the new fashions—if you can call them that— she's modelling. Everything is dark or baggy, but always scruffy. She even chopped off her hair and dyed it blue-black herself a few weeks ago. We've always had the same long brown hair. Somehow, teachers still can't tell us apart.

7. Interest in witchcraft.

Just last weekend I saw her holding a seance at a slumber party I was excluded from. Perched at the top of the basement stairs, I watched her and her friends call on the spirits to get revenge on Daniela Hendrick because she tattled on them for ditching math. They were cackling like a coven, gathered around candles while they did their wicked ritual. I ran away after that, but who knows what else they did? They may have summoned Bloody Mary or cursed someone for all I know.

She also has tons of black candles and a tarot deck in her bedroom. She scrawls pentagrams on all her notebooks and draws other wicked sigils on her skin with markers like tattoos. This might mean her connection to the darkness is growing which is not a good sign.

8. Aversion to the sacred.

She refuses to go to church with us anymore. She screamed the most heretical things about the corruption and contradictions of organized religion. Mom has let her stop coming to Sunday service, likely to stop the screaming. In an attempt to protect her, I put a crucifix on her door only to find it inverted the next day with a vile quote from *The Exorcist* pinned next to it.

9. Changes in behavior.

We used to be inseparable. We might as well have been conjoined twins because we did everything together, but lately, she wants nothing to do with me. Maybe it's because I can see her for what she truly is. She's angry all the time and constantly itching to start a fight over nothing. She's stopped trying at school. If she goes to class at all, she's never done the homework and doesn't show up to the detentions she's frequently assigned. If there's a rule, she seems to want to break it: she steals from stores, cheats on tests, breaks curfew, and doesn't follow the school dress code. As someone who believes in the virtue of justice, I find her behavior abhorrent and senseless.

I look at the pages of evidence I've produced. It all adds up to one thing in my mind—demonic possession. I have hope—another virtue of mine—that I can save her. I vow, here and now, to cure her.

Summer

My stranger of a sister is squatting at the front of the bus, scribbling furiously into her notebook. I know she's secretly watching me as I hang with my new friends at the back of the bus. Yeah, the gang are kinda known as burnouts, but they're nice and accepted me immediately when Autumn started to withdraw. They introduced me to some awesome music and Anna gave me a makeover, which I think looks cool, but I mostly let her do it so I could spend time with her and away from my uncomfortable house. Mom was not pleased. She said, "You look like a punk!"

I was like, "Yeah, that's the point."

Since I started to hang with the group, I kinda started dating one of the guys, Grady. He's cute, darkly sarcastic in a way that makes me laugh or think about shit in a new way and is teaching me to play the guitar. I also make out with the super-hot Anna sometimes. I think I like it better. Girls are softer and not fragile in a way that is so fucking satisfying. No one seems to care that

I'm hooking up with both of them. Everyone in the gang seems to have hooked up at some point, so they're kinda casual about it all. Maybe that's part of why I like being with them—because they're cool and relaxed while everything at home and school is tense and serious.

I needed these guys when Autumn abandoned me and started doing her super-freak impression because I'd never felt more alone. It was lonely in a way I can't even describe. I'd never done anything by myself my whole life, not even gestate. I was so hurt at first, I started doing some things just to feel something.

I sneak out on school nights to get drunk and high in the park because it's fun and makes me forget the chilling atmosphere at home. I even lost my virginity to see if I'd feel close to someone again. It wasn't a big deal, not like everyone says anyway. I feel kinda weird about it though because me and my sister had this dumb promise about saving ourselves for marriage, and I think she knows I broke our pact. I really want to tell Autumn—she'd probably call it 'confession'—like I would have a few months ago, but that girl isn't there anymore.

We turn to look at one another in unison; the only thing we've done together in ages.

Autumn

Because she's bad I have to be virtuous enough for both of us, and I have faith—another virtue I keep—that this will help expel the demon from Summer.

When we sit down to dinner, my sister scarfs down her spaghetti at a disgusting rate. Her appetite has changed lately. Mom attributes it to a growth spurt, but I know it's because she's eating for two and feeding her little demon.

"Autumn?" Mom asks, "Why aren't you eating, honey?"

It's partly because Summer's gluttony makes me feel sick but mostly, I am making a great sacrifice for her sake. "I'm fasting," I reply.

"That's dangerous," says Mom. "I hope it's not a peer pressure thing, honey, because you're perfect just as you are."

"It's for mortification," I say.

"What is that? Some new fad us old folks wouldn't understand?" Mom asks.

"It's penance for sin performed through the body," I say, disappointed Mom may not be as devoted as me.

"That's some real stupid shit," adds Summer, before declaring she is done and excusing herself without clearing her plate like Mom asks because she's already gone before the words come out. I clear all our plates, including my full one, my stomach rumbling for a good cause.

Summer

Music has become my lifeline. I choke down family dinners so I can get the fuck out of that dysfunctional situation and escape to the comfort and chaos of my new friends or into something more creative and transportive. With lyrics, I can express all my confusion, and when I wail on the strings of my guitar, I can find a pace and melody that releases the hurt and anger. It's my damn religion, a way to purge the feelings that bite too hard.

When I think I've got something, I pick up the phone, no matter how late it is, and call Grady or Anna. They listen to me, like, really listen, the way Autumn used to. Tonight, I've got one about how my sister has changed and deserted me wrapped not too neatly in a death metaphor. Grady likes how I switch from staccato to stormy strumming. He says, "It's, like, I can feel you going through different stages of grief."

Anna likes the lyrics, saying, "They're melancholic one minute and malicious the next. It feels real and honest." It is honest, and that they get it gives me the feeling of being connected to someone again when my most meaningful connection has been brutally severed.

I open my window and lean out as I light up a joint to celebrate and help me sleep. It's been hard to sleep when I know the girl in the next room is a stranger who gives me sinister stares all day and has shown she's willing to fuck with me in ways that are borderline harmful.

Autumn

When Summer is done with her noise-making for the night, I visit her room. I've been trying to catch her levitating. It's a sign that possession is progressing to a fully integrated level. Right now, I think there's still some Summer in there, but for how long? When I open the door, she's smoking marijuana and immediately bites my head off. It's the monster in her snapping at me. The aggression likely conjured by the smoking. I read somewhere that mind-altering substances can act as a conduit to dark forces, so I ask, "Are you hearing voices?" She responds with a string of insults, quite stunning in their vulgarity.

Refusing to internalize her demonic hate, I look around her room in disgust. Her bed is a mess. The floor is covered with tapes, CDs, magazines, and dirty clothing. Underneath the illegal herbs, I can smell sweat. The entire scene reminds me of sloth, and I add another sin to her growing list.

She violently pushes me out the door, slamming it in my face. She can't lock me out forever. I'm coming for the devil inside her.

Summer

My door flings open. I drop my spliff to the sill in a panic and turn to see August, leaning against the doorframe with her arms crossed and a stern look on her face. "Holy shit, dude," I say. "Ever hear of knocking?!"

"Are you done playing your Satanic music for the night so the rest of us can get some sleep?" she asks.

"Yes, and now I'm cleansing the room with herbs," I say, picking up my joint and taking a puff.

My sister tuts and waves her hand in front of her face with disgust. "That stuff will warp your mind."

"That's the idea," I reply, turning my back on her to blow smoke out the window.

"It's a psychedelic, you know," she says. "Does it make you hear voices?"

I turn back to her, and she's deadly serious. "I hear your voice right now and, frankly, it's freaking me out."

"Is it how you speak with the Devil?" she asks. I have no idea what to say to this because she's not joking, and I've got a buzz and only jokes. "The Lord speaks to me when I pray. He's worried for your immortal soul, and so am I."

"Enough with the Jesus crap," I snap. "It creeps me out. Actually, can you just get out? You're bringing me down with your new holier-than-thou persona." She spins on her heels and practically floats away without closing the door. I rush to slam the door and contain the pot smell in my room. With smoke spilling out my window, I shudder at how chilling the eerie calm of Autumn's new demeanour is, paired with the preachy, pious words that come out of her mouth. I pick up my phone and start searching: *'Signs someone is in a cult.'*

Autumn

The drugs make her sleepy, so I don't have to wait too long to sneak back in and check on her. She's fast asleep, half spilling out of the covers and breathing heavily. Staring at my heathen sister, she looks so comfortable carrying her demon, and I know I will have to atone for this. I go back to my room and sprinkle sand at my bedside. Kneeling into it, I say my nightly prayers. With the grains digging into my knees, I ask that the Lord help me heal my sister, and I feel his reassuring presence flowing through me. It tells me that I am on the right path with my work on the Summer problem.

As mortification on behalf of my possessed sister, slumbering sweetly next door, I lay on the floor with no pillow or blanket, hugging my bible and attempting to sleep.

Summer

I pretend to sleep when my sister sneaks back into my room a little while later. It's not the first time she's spied on me lately and, honestly, it's freaky. With my lights out, there's just her silhouette in the dim glow of the light snaking up the stairs from the living room where our mom is still watching TV. She's always unsettlingly still. She doesn't enter. She doesn't do anything but watch me for a minute or so and then slink away, quietly closing the door behind her.

Once she's gone, I throw the covers over my head, grab my flashlight and flick through a magazine quiz to test if someone you know is in a cult.

1. Obsession with a group, person, or set of ideas.

Ever since Dad left, she seemed to find solace in her faith. I thought it was healthy at first, but now she's muttering biblical verses, scolding me for my lack of virtue, and calling out my 'sins' like it's her only purpose in the world. That smacks of obsession to me.

2. Perceiving criticism as persecution.

Autumn's whole thing was getting to me, so I tried to tell Mom—a total jerk move, I know—to get her off my back. Autumn must have found out I ratted on her because that night when I'd crawled through my window way after curfew, she was waiting for me, sat still as a rock on my bed. She scared the living shit out of me. I fell into my room, making more noise than I'd have liked to when she started her lecture. She didn't even look at me, just recited a bunch of crap about sinners and demons always trying to tear down the righteous. Even stoned out of my mind, I knew which side I was supposedly on in this speech.

3. Relying on their source for thoughts.

She seems to think The Bible has the answers to everything. A few weeks ago, when Mom was stressing over the bills, Autumn laid her hand on her shoulder like a preacher and said, "And my God will supply every need of yours according to his riches in glory in Christ Jesus, Philippians 4:19." I was like, "Can we ask Phillip to pay the mortgage?" No one thought it was funny and Mom even thanked her for the support.

While Mom might be indulging her, the kids at school are not so kind. She scribbles her Jesus shit on her notebooks and even challenged Mr. Kaur in Physics class one time when we were talking about expansion theory.

Out of nowhere, no hand raised, she just cooly declared, "In the beginning God created the heavens and the earth. Now the earth was formless and empty, darkness was over the surface of the deep, and the Spirit of God was hovering over the waters. And God said, 'Let there be light,' and there was light. Genesis 1:1-3." The whole class laughed at her. I joined in. I'm not immune to peer pressure and can be an ass sometimes, but I was mostly concerned for her.

4. Disdain for people who have left the community.

Her weirdness towards me really started when I stopped attending church. I just wasn't into it, hated getting up early on a Sunday, and the prospect of having two hours to myself was just too appealing. Sue me. But she called me a sinner instead, stopped talking to me and started watching and judging my every move. Having a stalker who is the mirror image of you is pretty damn disconcerting. It almost feels like non-consensual self-loathing.

It's all adding up; Autumn has been seriously seduced by the cult of religion. How do I even begin to deal with that?

Autumn

I wait with my ear to the wall until 3 a.m. when I hear her stumble through the window. She's especially late, and we'll both be tired tomorrow. She is not being as quiet as usual, telling me she's drunk. The demon in her must have been thirsty tonight. Then I hear her crying. Do demons feel things? Why would a host be crying?

Thinking on it, the only logical conclusion is that it's a trap meant to lure me to her for some nefarious reason. I won't fall for it. Maybe the demon has corrupted her body and is looking for a new one to infect. The demon might have developed a certain hunger for blood, violence, or terror. The tears are a bad omen. I will have to pray for guidance, that this isn't the ultimate phase of possession, and it's not too late to save Summer's soul.

Summer

I'm drunk. I shouldn't have gotten this drunk, but I had a garbage day and needed to escape my mind and body for a bit. The beer and tequila combination has made me clumsy, so I stumble around, crashing into my dresser. Even with the numb of the buzz, I feel it, and it makes me cry. I'm also crying for everything else and not trying to conceal my sobs, hoping that my sister will hear in the next room and, despite our recent distance, come to comfort me because I really need her right now.

I wake up alone, feeling like shit. I must have cried myself to sleep, and Autumn neglected me. It makes the tears flow again. Then my stomach churns, my mouth waters and I bolt for the bathroom to blow chunks.

Autumn

Now Summer is sick. She's been throwing up all morning. Our mother is holding her hair back and trying to comfort her while she bats her away. "Piss off, Mom," she croaks. "This is fucking gross, and I don't need your help."

Not leaving her demonic side, Mom asks me to fetch some water for my sister. I wish I had holy water, so I pour a glass and chant a blessing over it, hoping it will make a difference. "Blessed are you, Lord, all-powerful God, who in Christ, the living water of salvation, blessed and transformed us. Grant that we will be refreshed inwardly by the power of the Holy Spirit."

Mom comes out of the bathroom looking hurt and worried. I'm worried too, but for different reasons. I'm concerned this is her body trying to reject the demon, or the demon intentionally and gleefully causing her pain, or that her head is going to spin around. This is the most serious of her symptoms yet and nothing I have done to compensate for or intervene in her possession seems to be working. She is still the moody, mean, and lazy beast she's been for months, and now she's puking pea soup. I deem it prudent—my most practiced virtue—to get serious and do some research. While doing my charitable—a great virtue—volunteer shift at the library, I collect books from the Theology section on demons and demonic possession. My efforts to cure Summer so far have been too broad. I need to find out precisely which demon is possessing her so I can tackle it head-on.

When I get home, Summer is a sweaty mess, moaning and groaning from her bed between trips to the bathroom. I take my books to my room and start my research. None of the seven—Lucifer, Mammon, Asmodeus, Leviathan, Beelzebub, Satan, or Belphgor—seem to fit her afflictions. Each is tied to a specific sin, and she's been indulging in them all. I flip through all manner of demons: the four princes of the elements, the four princes of the spirits, and the three infernal judges. None seem right. Then I find the Furies, three femme demons.

Summer

I feel like crap all day, and Mom doesn't even try to make me go to school. I stay in bed, a sweaty, disgusting mess who was put into her pyjamas by her mother like a child. I'm not even sure I brushed my teeth. I definitely haven't washed my face, so yesterday's make-up is smudged into a monstrous formation. I hear Grady knock at my bedroom window. If he's here, school must be out, which means I've been lying in my own filth for hours. After last night I don't want to see him, but I also want him to hold me and fix everything.

I slide the window open and dive back into my bed, hiding my hideous face in the covers. He doesn't say anything for a while, then we say everything. We repeat the things we said last night and so much more. It doesn't solve anything. I'm not sure anything can. He climbs onto the bed and envelops me in his arms. We stay like that silently until Autumn crashes in.

Autumn

I check on my Fury of a sister, and she's in bed with a boy after doing who knows what. He looks exhausted and slightly sad. She looks furious. I wonder if the demon has worked its wicked magic on him. While I have no particular feelings for a burnout like Grady Maddox, it's my duty to warn him.

"Stay away from her," I say.

"Get out!" Summer screams. She looks awful. I don't move, so she moves me. Grabbing my arms with strength that can only be from the thing inside her, she tells him to stay put and violently drags me to my room where she gives me a verbal thrashing full of her flaming language and blasphemes, which make me cringe. Now I know what she is, she doesn't frighten me, because her kind is not out to hurt me. I'm not her type. I stand calmly and say, "I see you, and you don't scare me. 'No harm comes to the godly, but the wicked have their fill of trouble.' Proverbs 12:21." Rage fills her mottled face, and she storms out.

I have work to do. I'm so close to the cure.

Summer

My sister acts all virtuous, but she's just a heinous bitch. She can't even see how desperate and hurt I am. She just gave me her cold eyes and biblical nonsense when my heart was screaming at her for help.

Back in my room, Grady is sat on the bed, holding my snake. He heard everything and accused me of losing it.

"I think I have every right to be losing it right now," I reply.

"That ain't gonna fix anything," he says. "I'm gonna jet. Call me when you've mellowed, alright." And with that, he climbs back out my window, and the answer comes to me: losing it will actually fix everything.

Autumn

I'm poring over the only book I could find featuring The Furies that I checked out of the library. If they weren't fiends, they'd be fascinating. They are creatures of vengeance, sinister sisters interested only in pursuing wrongdoers, especially men. I am clear on that count, but Grady isn't. Which reminds me that, since I found them in bed together, they'd probably done it. I'll have the self-flagellate to repent on her behalf tonight.

Now that I'm not directly concerned for my safety, I need to work out how to get this thing out of my sister. It'll still take courage—the only virtue I have yet to master—to take on this task. Tearing through the pages of my book, I come across a section of female Saints. There are more of them than I would have thought. They are beautiful and literal perfection. Their images practically shine off the page, calling to me, making my body hum... or are they humming? I can see myself in them.

I look at the miracles these women have performed, anointing them to sainthood. Bilocation: I have a twin, so I am, in a way, always in two places at one time. Levitation: I had associated this with the demonic and possessed. Jumping as high as I can, I see if the air can catch me and make me float. I fail. This will not be my miracle. Stigmata: of all the miracles, this is the one I wish for the most. As a mirror of Christ, it seems the holiest. I take a red marker and draw dots on my wrists, feet and side, closing my eyes and trying to feel his suffering in me and summon forth actual blood. Nothing. My body is clean. Healings: Healings! This will be my miracle as I cure my sister of the demon that plagues her. I just need the method for an exorcism and the courage to confront her, and I will be exalted.

Summer

I rummage through Mom's liquor cabinet, looking for some hair of the dog. I've gotta take the worst of the shit that she won't miss, so schnapps is my poison. I smuggle the bottle to my room, climb out my window to the roof, and start chugging. The blubbering quickly follows. My mind spirals with just how fucked everything is. I wish I had the courage to go to my sister and tell her everything: how I've been feeling these past months, and just how much I need and miss her. She'd know what to do. Somehow, it's easier to find the courage to do the terrible thing I'm about to do.

As it turns out, I don't need to find the courage to make sisterly contact because she does. She pokes her head out of the window and smiles at me for the first time in an eternity.

Autumn

I carefully crawl to the beast masquerading as my sister over the old roof tiles. Sitting next to her, I pull my knees up and wrap my arms around them. I'm not nervous. I have courage and all the other virtues with me.

"You've been going through some changes recently," I say. "Don't think I haven't noticed just because we're not close anymore."

Through tears that I can only imagine are crocodiles because demons feel nothing that would provoke such an emotional reaction, she replies, "No shit, Sherlock."

"I know what's going on," I say, "and I can help you."

"You can?" she replies, and I think I see genuine Summer and relief in her eyes.

Exchanging her near-empty bottle for a bottle of water I've blessed, properly this time with all my virtues intact. I tell her to drink.

Sniffing it, she says, "This is just water. What will it do other than hydrate me?"

"It's not just water," I say. "I've done my research. It will expel that thing inside you."

Putting a hand on her belly, she takes a reluctant sip. Then she drinks more. I nod in encouragement and utter the exorcism prayer under my breath.

"What?" she asks.

"Nothing," I reply. "I'm just saying a little prayer for you. Praying that it will work."

She finishes the bottle and hands it back to me. Nothing seems to be happening. I was expecting something dramatic from the movies I've seen—screaming, swearing, convulsions, violent outbursts, but she seems peaceful. Summer looks more relaxed than I've seen her in months. Maybe that is how it happens—a whimper, not a bang.

"Do you feel anything?" I ask.

"I feel..." she pauses to think. "I feel ready." I don't know what this means, but she stands on drunk legs, holding her arms out. Her pose reminds me of the crucifixion. "I'm ready to make sure it's finished," she says before leaping from the roof.

I must have weakened the Fury enough for Summer to want it out of herself.

Summer

Falling is easy. Gravity does all the work. I crash to the ground from our second story. It's not enough to kill me, but it should do the damage I need. I feel bones crack and flesh pierce on sticks and rocks, but I feel no pain, only relief. I realize that I can't move. I think it's just from the shock and not broken bones. There's warmth and stickiness. I can't move to look but I assume it's blood pooling in various places and, thankfully, the place I want most. It makes me smile. My extreme cure was effective. "It worked," I scream to the skies.

Autumn

I look down at my sister's still body on the ground. There's quite a lot of blood, but I'm not worried. That's probably her purging the Fury. Plus, she's smiling and looks peaceful. She yells up to me, "It worked!"

I've done it. I've cured her. I look up to the heavens and wait for my ascension.

Outro

Content warnings: Alcohol use, suggested self-induced abortion.

Sainthood is my favorite Tegan and Sara record. It represents their transition from their folky origins to gay pop. It's weird, and I adore it. The album title, the song *The Cure*, and the twins themselves inspired this story. The lyrics suggest wanting to fix a toxic relationship. In this tale, that relationship is between twins. Tegan and Sara have spoken about growing apart in their autobiography, *High School*, as well as the tensions that come from working together. I frame that tension in possession as an allegory for the angst of teendom and the physical and emotional changes of pregnancy. This is the only work in this collection that uses dual perspective because in their writings—including songs which they write separately—they tell their stories from their perspective, reminding us that while they may look alike, they are individuals. Here, that structure helps emphasize that they are on extremely different wavelengths and gives them space to be who they are and struggle in their own ways. To be clear, these twins are not representations of Tegan or Sara, and I am not suggesting either of them is evil.

With inspiration from the inventors of queer pop, I certainly wanted the story to be more queer. While there are nods to Summer's sexual orientation, I have personally struggled with my sexuality and the possessive qualities of compulsory heteronormativity which are present in this 'possession' story. I sincerely hope that this does not come off as disrespect to the work that Tegan and Sara have done for the LGBTQ2S+ communities.

Got A Man

I don't see his blonde girl again after he escorts her from the bar. When he returns, he says she's an ex who was stalking him, but she had to barf, and he felt obliged to help her out.

What a good fucking guy.

I've been onto him since he walked in. I know he's the asshole who's been sending fucked up anatomy to the morgue every summer for years.

I don't know this through the news. That shit isn't publicized because it would freak people out. Even though he is a hazard to the public, the mortals of science don't know what is causing the gruesome deaths and the politicians don't know how to 'spin' the mystery, so they just keep it quiet while beautiful girls die screaming.

I can't believe I've found him. Actually, he kind of fell into my lap while on one of my regular prowls. Jacob doesn't know it, but he's my new toy. I've got a man to kill. But first, I'm gonna make him want to die.

He flirts like a professional. He's supremely cool, with the perfect blend of genuine-appearing attentiveness and precision negging. He uses his stormy blue eyes like mesmerizing crystals. If I was any regular woman, I'd be halfway to obsessed— or at least flat on my back— by now.

I'd be impressed if I wasn't better.

I'm not turning it on just yet, though. That's not how you capture a beast like this. I'm playing the part of helpless prey: flipping my ebony hair, wearing a dreamy expression in my green eyes, laughing coyly on cue, and finding any excuse to gently lay hands on him. He's buying it like he's buying my drinks.

I anticipate he will make an excuse to leave early and leave me wanting more. I'm correct and must perform a desire for him to stay and feign disappointment when he won't budge. Then I pretend to be awkward with a touch of desperation when I contrive a reason to get his number. He gives it to me as though it is a gift, and I nearly make myself sick when I text him a kiss emoji before he's out of sight.

I watch as he pauses to reply with a winky face. He, predictably, leaves without looking back.

***

Jacob courts me into boredom with quaint shit like carnivals and picnics. I act delighted and display appropriate amounts of desire with kisses and simple sex that exclusively serves his needs. I have to be careful with the intimacy because I'm innately insatiable in that department. Seduction is my superpower. And it is a very useful one when my objective is to destroy.

On our third date, he tells me not to fall in love with him. That won't be a problem for me. It's the start of the problems for him, though.

133

At first, I work hard to cover up my listlessness. Once he thinks he's got his claws firmly into me, I slowly introduce apathy and distaste for his date ideas, reject his public advances, and reduce my effort in the bedroom.

His blue eyes grow confused. He could just give up and move on to his next victim, but beasts like him don't lose.

Now I must endure him ratcheting up acts to tempt me. He plays guitar and piano for me with a passion that I am impervious to. I am sure to appear disinterested while listening, then praise it lightly. He tries taking me to a ball game which I yawn through. He attempts to awe me with his fake selfless, charitable side by taking me to a gala with a $1500 per-head dinner—he emphasizes the cost—with proceeds going to some museum or gallery and not an actual cause.

I am even invited to his apartment, which I am sure he has redecorated in a clean mid-century style to impress me. While there, he gives me a tiresome, in-depth tour of the unique items and features of his home and highlights that I am the first woman he's ever invited over because he doesn't want anyone to get too attached. He sticks to his 'no love' schtick even now, not realizing how the tables have turned, and he's the one begging for affection.

After a couple of weeks, Jacob asks me what is wrong with genuine confusion. He knows that my heart should be aching for him—quite literally—by now. If I had a heart, it might be. Now I know it is time to activate my plans. I shrug and suggest that we see other people. I gleefully watch him squirm to keep his cool as he agrees.

But he does not agree this is how it should be for a guy like him and makes sure to monopolize my nights. It's exactly what I want. Not because I want to spend time with the monster, but because it gives me the opportunity to start my own deadly seduction.

One night after his standard missionary—men like him like being on top, in control, and don't feel the need to pleasure or

impress because you should be grateful to have them on and in
you— I tell him I am bored with our sex life. He is stunned and
fails to hide it. He swears he has never had any complaints about
his sexual prowess before and will try anything to satisfy me and
suggests a weekend getaway. It is precisely what I need to hear.

***

I make him do all the coordination for our trip to East Hampton
and provide mellow responses to all his plans. They are plans I
am sure girls have died for because he arranges the most
romantic few days, plan which had probably been suggested to
him and rejected by him in his previous courtships. I will be
using the dream weekend of his dead girls to enact my
vengeance with fucking poetry and no romance.

***

We arrive at a gorgeous beachfront cottage that his other girls
would kill for. He now has a kicked-puppy quality to him and
constantly asks if everything is to my liking. I can genuinely say
it is because I'm in control now, and his nightmare is about to
begin.

I remind him that we are here to focus on my pleasure, so he
asks how I want to 'make love.' The words are clearly foreign to
him, but my sick seduction tears them from his lips. I hope that
I have not completely neutered him so that he can't perform,
because that is essential to my ritual.

I make demands, and he enthusiastically complies. My sex is
beguiling him like he brutally bewitched his victims. When he's
naked and vulnerable, I begin my vengeance on him during
some degradation play.

"You're a real asshole," I say.

He agrees and seems surprised his body responds to the
insult.

135

"You wanna know just how big an asshole you are?" I ask, firmly placing my hand on his buttocks. He nods his head, getting visibly more excited.

"This big!" I declare and start to apply pressure. Sinking my nails into the taught flesh of his glutes my fingers press down the crevasse between them, spreading him wide. There it is. The tight puckering pink mass of sinew and muscle that is his asshole and the thing that he creates in others. He seems nervous now and with words of fierce degradation, I tear his cheeks apart with such force I rip his anus wide open, splitting his rectum, and spilling the contents of his colon. What was a crack is now a grotesque cavern and my amends for all his wrongdoings.

That's when the screaming and bleeding begins.

Jacob falls to the floor, trying desperately to hold himself together. I sigh and kneel beside him. Coldly, I tell him I don't like what he does to women, and it is time he gets a taste of how it feels.

"I don't know exactly what kind of monster you are or how you do it, so we're just going to have to approximate and improvise," I say, patting him roughly on the back and making him wail.

"Don't do this," he pleads.

"Is that what they say?" I ask. I answer my own question. "No. I don't suppose they do because you play a slow, painful game that they aren't even aware of—"

"I'm sorry," he cries. "I don't mean to—"

"And yet, you do," I reply. "Again and again." I bear down on him, looking him in the eyes so he can see how serious I am. "Your victims may not be aware, but I want you aware. Nice and aware until I'm done."

"What are you?" he asks.

I tell him I'm just like him, only worse.

His eyes are wide and filled with fear and tears. I am unmoved, and with my long nails, I bore into his back, tearing him a new one. Then another, and another, and another. My crimson-covered fingers dig into his flesh over and over with delight. It's not as though we need more assholes in the world but the justice is poetic.

He has thirteen assholes before he begs for me to kill him.

I will.

But only when he's got a gaping hole for each of his girls.

Outro

Content warnings: Toxic relationships, revenge, gore, body horror.

"I got a man who makes me wanna kill," is the opening lyric for *Man* by the Yeah Yeah Yeahs from their debut album, *Fever To Tell*. Singer, Karen O practically screams these words repeatedly with the pain of a scorned woman. I've hollered along many times and it's like a spell to release rage. Step away from the meditation and give it a try. Seriously.

From the tone and lyrics of the song, I knew it had to be a revenge story and having already written *Summer (L)over*; I decided to connect the two and take the opportunity for some poetic justice for the antagonist who callously wins the hearts of women to break them most brutally. While equally brutal, this collection needed a 'good for her' moment. This is most definitely that, in the ugly way I've loved about this literary trend.

Soul Stowaway

The first time I spoke to Marigold she was hanging upside down on the old monkey bars in the Honey Glades park. Her little feet were hooked under the adjacent bar to stop her falling, her school skirt fell over her shoulders, and the house key around her neck dangled precariously.

I asked her what she was doing, and she said she was playing vampires. I was only ten years old and didn't know what that meant. She explained, pretending to be exasperated by my know-nothing self, but I could tell she was actually excited to show off her knowledge. She told me vampires were like bats. They hung from trees with their cape or wings wrapped around them as a disguise. She pulled her skirt around herself to demonstrate. Continuing, she described how they waited for unsuspecting prey—preferably stupid-face boys—to walk past and then they would swoop down and attack them. They would suck all the blood from them and that blood made them live forever and ever.

I said that was gross and asked how they could do something like that. Flipping down from the bars, she shrugged and said, "Because they don't have souls."

"Do you have a soul?" I asked.

"Yeah," she replied. "I'm just playing vampires, dummy. I'm not really one."

"What's your soul made of?" I asked.

She thought for a second and replied, "Asbestos."

I didn't understand what that meant, but that's how I became best friends with the wild girl whose soul was composed of crystals that were impervious to corrosion and dangerous with prolonged exposure.

She asked me if I wanted to learn to avoid vampire attacks, and I said I did. Garlic and crosses helped but you could escape their clutches if you swung really, really high. We must have spent an hour pumping our legs furiously on the swings to get height and kick away vampires pursuing us.

I asked why this worked, and she said it was because they'd mistake us for flying witches, and they didn't drink stinking witch blood.

I watched her leap from the swing from an intimidating height. She flew through the air, sticking the landing at the edge of the woodlands bordering the North of the park. She screeched and flapped her arms, calling me over.

I was too much of a scaredy-cat to jump, so I slammed my feet down, burning rubber on the concrete to slow my sway to a stop. At the park perimeter—and the trees I was forbidden to pass but would many times with Marigold's encouragement—there were dozens of tiny frogs hopping about. She declared this was evidence that shithead trolls were roaming the woods. In that moment, I understood why my parents didn't want me playing beyond the trees. I didn't want to run into any trolls. I knew nothing of danger back then.

A tired-looking woman marched to the park gates and hollered Marigold's name, demanding she get home immediately for supper and warning she better not have dirtied her school uniform. Her uniform was rumpled and dusty. Marigold turned to me and made a barfing face.

"Looks like the nag hag is home." She sighed. "I gotta go or she'll shit a brick, but see you here tomorrow?"

"Sure," I said, watching her hop away to her own strange rhythm. She got distracted by rocks along the way and I heard her mother scold her then her sass back something about looking for the perfect stone to slay a dragon unless she wanted to get burned to a crisp in their hellfire breath. I would never dream of talking to my parents like that, but her mother rolled her eyes, laughed and half-hugged, half-dragged her home.

We played together at the park every day after school for the rest of the school year and summer. We always played monsters. She knew so many different kinds: zombies, succubi, witches, nymphs, wicked fairies, trolls, werewolves, urges, goblins, mummies, banshees, sirens, and dragons. We played them all. This was before we knew about real monsters.

I'd never met anyone like Marigold. She was fearless and knew things no one else our age did—not important things; odd stuff. She swore at least every other sentence, using words I'd never heard of. She called Thomas H a dildo to his face when he interrupted us casting a spell on the witch finder general. I learned the words dickwad and fucknut when the Patel twins made fun of us for howling to scare away werewolves before the full moon. She even gave her older brother shit when he and his friends came to smoke the funny-smelling cigarettes in the park. She'd tell stories about him pissing himself as a kid and something about him having hairy palms. She didn't do it just to be mean or to defend herself. It seemed to amuse her, and I was fascinated by how she couldn't care less what anyone thought.

One day, we found a fairy ring growing on the edge of the park field. To me, it looked like a small circle of ugly mushrooms. She was adamant that we were fae fighters and must destroy it carefully or else we'd be lured into the fairy realm where they would imprison us and drive us mad. There were boys playing football on the field and the ball came whizzing in our direction, hitting me in the back of the head. It stung and stunned me into silence while the boys laughed, but

Marigold had plenty to say. Cussing them out, she threw their ball into the stream where the trolls lived. The boys were mad and insisted she go get their ball back. She shrugged, saying she'd get their ball before marching over to one of them and kicking him in the groin. She declared poetic justice as he doubled over, eyes watering. His friends helped him up and yelled empty threats as they walked away. She'd already won but finished them off with a string of insults, calling all boys wicked, dumbasses, mouth breathers with butts for brains.

Having saved us from the wicked boys, she got back to work demolishing the fairy circle and saving our souls from the paranormal wicked creatures.

***

By the end of that summer, we were eleven and too old for the old games. We were off to a new school and had to grow up a bit. Marigold didn't lose any of her love for monsters, though. They were the subject of her art projects, English assignments, and she argued with the teachers when they gave her low grades for what she thought was perfect work. Marigold got particularly excited when we studied Greek mythology. It was full of monsters even she didn't know about. Gorgons became her new goddesses. She didn't pay attention to any of her other classes. If there were no monsters, she wasn't interested.

She was also seeing monsters everywhere. Painting my nails with white correction fluid I'd have to pick off on the way home, she explained that the popular girls were zombies, mindlessly doing whatever was decided was cool. The nerds were vampires, sucking up to teachers and gobbling up good grades, and the jock guys were trolls with their ridiculous muscles and brainless displays of violence playing pointless sports.

She wasn't shy about letting people know she didn't like them, so everyone labelled her weird. No one really hassled her, though. Probably because her big brother, Felix, was cool. She could have stood up for herself, but it was a non-issue. I was still

142

in awe of how herself she was. I had no idea who I was unless I was next to her, even if that made me weird by association.

We were just as close—more so—by thirteen, at which point we were eating dinner at each other's houses every night and having sleepovers all weekend. My parents were less than impressed that my only friend was so strange and from 'one of those families,' the ones that lived in the duplexes and weren't didn't have as much money as the rest of this snotty town. I thought they were the strange ones. They were so boring and ordinary while Marigold's house was glorious chaos. There was always noise, whether it was some kind of row over who didn't do chores, siblings chasing and teasing each other up and down the house, or everyone talking over one another at the dinner table. The place was alive, and Marigold was its beating heart. She was constantly pushing buttons by teaching her baby sister foul language; giving the kid matches to play with; announcing she was pregnant or possessed by a demon; telling on Felix for smoking and having moron buddies; or mocking her mother's current boyfriend with wit and ease. It would always cause a ruckus, but they loved and accepted her ways.

I was in love with her room. It had her personality all over it: her drawings of otherworldly creatures plastered the walls, the duvet cover she'd tried to dye black but wound up dark grey with lighter splotches, and all her furniture was covered with crude graffiti or symbols and words she described as 'wards' and 'incantations.' It was here that we made an oath. She said I was the only one who really understood her, that we were kindred spirits, soulmates. She wanted to bind us together forever using that occult knowledge I never understood how she'd acquired.

The ritual was simple; a few words and drops of blood. We scraped a protractor down our palms until we broke the skin, then clasped our hands together and laid their impressions on the wall. For the rest of our lives, there were two distinct, but entwined, red palm prints over her bed. We must have slept under that sigil of our connected souls together hundreds of nights.

***

By the time we were fifteen, Marigold was still herself, but her boldness had taken her in new directions. She was a dedicated goth now. My parents would never allow me to dress all in black, cake myself in dark make-up or get piercings, so I did my own soft version and wiped the eyeliner away before going home. She also started seeing guys. Even the kind she'd deemed monstrous. They were rarely from our school, mostly older and drove cars. Part of me didn't like it, not because I was jealous but because I missed her. The other part of me was exhilarated because I got to live vicariously, learning all about her exploits when she'd creep in my window after dark and tell me all the gory details or quietly cry while I held her when the monsters were mean to her heart.

There was this one guy who kept coming up—Wes. She was convinced he was an incubus. Sometimes this was a good thing because he made her feel irresistibly out of control and set her whole body on fire. Other times it was a bad thing and he was sucking the life out of her, which I could see from the bruise-like hickies on her neck and because she couldn't even muster the energy or ire to curse about him. On those occasions, it was like he'd snuffed the fire he set in her out.

The whole thing was confusing to me so I decided that, as soulmates, I needed to get back in sync with her and that meant exploring my sexuality so I could understand her. When I told her I was ready—I wasn't sure that I was—she was alive and wild again. She started selecting candidates for me. Obviously, zombies and trolls were out of the question, but a vampire might be okay because geeks were 'attainable' and 'gagging for it.' I didn't want a monster of any kind and passed on all her suggestions.

Just as we were running out of potential dates, Marigold was
giddy that Wes and some of his friends were having a party on
the weekend and it would be at the park we used to play
monsters in all those years ago.

"It's fucking fate," she said. "You're gonna lose it where we
met." She raved that it was a cunting cosmic sign, some bloody
omen, and more proof that we were true soulmates.

***

I let her dress me for the big night and was more nervous than
I've ever been in my entire life as we walked past the empty
space where the rusted monkey bars and approached a gang of
rowdy rocker guys. Marigold pointed out three of them to avoid:
one because he was a straight-up asshole and demon, another
because he was cute but actually a walking STI, and the last
because he was Wes, and he belonged to her. The one she
pointed out as Wes called her name and before running to him,
she whispered, "Now go get 'em. Slut it up," in my ear.

I didn't know what to do without Marigold by my side. She
looked so at home with the older guys, huddled around a trash
can fire, listening to heavy music, smoking, drinking, and
laughing easily on Wes's lap. I heard the hiss beside me and
jumped out of my skin. I was fully prepared for it to be some
kind of snake demon we'd battled in this very spot a few years
ago, but when I turned, it was just Felix opening a can of beer.

"Shit," Marigold's brother said. "Didn't mean to scare ya.
Thought you heard me coming." He hands me the beer he just
popped, and I take it. It's not my first. We've swiped booze from
our parents plenty of times and I've never liked the taste of it,
but I think I'll need that buzz it gives me tonight.

"What are you doing here?" Felix asks.

I can't tell him the truth, so I swig from the can, borrow a bit
of his sister's sass and say, "What, like, is there some law against
it?"

145

He raises an eyebrow, knowing it's all bravado, and replies, "Just doesn't really seem like your scene."

It is so far from my scene, and I want to run away screaming. Then he sighs and throws an arm over my shoulder. It's nice and warm because Marigold didn't give me nearly enough to wear tonight. "Stick with me, kid," he says. "These guys will be all over you."

That was the whole point.

Felix guides me over to the group and introduces me to everyone. As I look around the guys and their fire-lit faces, all I see are monsters. The thought of any of them touching me is repulsive. I look to Marigold. Her eyes are bright with excitement and she's nodding her head towards the guys, encouraging me to go for it. I can't do it. Not even for my soulmate, and I plant myself with Felix on the outskirts of the group.

He's nice to me. He always has been aside from a little playful teasing, which always stung more than it should because I'm not strong like Marigold. Knowing us well, he asks what monsters his sister thinks all his friends are. I only know the three she warned me about earlier, so I diagnose the others myself from what she's taught me and the different dangerous vibes they give me in the dark. There's a Jekyll and Hyde type who lures you in with his looks and charm but will turn into a bastard beast the moment he's got you in his clutches. Felix laughs, saying that I nailed it. Then I point to the one I think of as Mephisto—a trickster demon—who will take advantage of the most desperate trying to make a deal that will always be to his advantage. I seem to have gotten it right again because he tells me he's a notorious lech with a talent for talking people into popping their cherries.

I really am surrounded by monsters.

"What do you make of Wes?" he asks. He stares at his sister, flirting with all her might and huffs, turning away.

"You don't like him?" I ask.

"Not with my sister," he replies.

"Did you tell her that?" I ask.

He snorts. "As if she listens to anything anyone says." It's true. Marigold is Marigold and she does what she wants, no matter how reckless. "So..."

"So what?" I reply.

"What kind of monster is he?" he asks again.

I tell him all about the incubus that we think Wes is. He's a sex demon who feeds off the romantic emotions and sexual energy of his victims, I explain. Felix crushes his can, tossing it with force before opening another immediately and giving me one, too.

"Crap," I say. "That was totally inappropriate. You don't wanna hear that kinda thing about your sister."

"It's nothing I didn't already know," he says. "Fuck!" He's pissed and can't take his angry eyes off the two as they fool around. "What kind of monster am I?"

I'm surprised by the question and not sure I want to find out the answer. I look at him closely. Unlike the other guys, he doesn't shapeshift in the flickering shadows of the fire. "I hate to break it to you," I say, "but you're no monster. Just a regular old human. Pretty rare around here." He turns to me, the rage leaving his eyes. Then he kisses me. It's more than a peck, but he doesn't try to devour me like other boys (monsters) would. When I part from his soft lips, I see Marigold glaring at us.

"What the absolute fuck?!" she says.

I've never upset Marigold before, but I've seen her ire and don't want to be on the receiving end of it. That wasn't an immediate problem because we hear the single pulse of a siren and the flashing lights at the park gates. Someone yells that it's the pigs and orders us to run. Felix takes my hand and we all head south, across the field to escape through the stream, splitting up as we hit the cul-de-sac on the other side. Running as fast as I can, I look behind me, seeing Marigold disappear in the opposite direction with Wes.

My parents would never let me stay out late so I was supposed to be staying at Marigold's. I couldn't go home at this hour dressed like this. They'd ground me for all eternity and never let me hang out with Marigold again, not that I was sure Marigold wanted to hang out with me after what I just did. Felix understands and walks me back to their place. I'm shaking the whole way, afraid of what my soulmate will say to me, and there's a deep, raw heat in my chest that isn't a panic attack. It feels like the soul that was entangled with mine for so long is pulling away.

I get into Marigold's familiar bed and place my hand on our bloody prints above the bed. It doesn't give me any comfort. I wait for her to return while preparing to take my licks and grovel, but she doesn't come back. She never came home again.

***

No one will tell me all the details, and I'm not sure if I'm grateful for it. It wasn't one of our monsters that got her in the end. It was just a man. Maybe that's the same thing. Everyone understood why I wouldn't speak for days, including Felix. The girl who flew right into my heart and soul was gone. I couldn't feel her anymore and it was agony, and I couldn't forgive myself for not being with her or that we never got to settle things. I thought that it should have been me instead of her. She was the strong one who was so alive and deserved life. The world wouldn't be that different without me, but it was dimmer without her. All my parents sad was that the soul never truly dies. With those words, in my pain and silence, I formulated the plan that would re-bind us.

On the day of her funeral—closed casket—I snuck into the Honey Glades funeral home and into her coffin. I could see the damage done to her. No wonder our souls were divided. Even our bond couldn't survive that violence. Maneuvering carefully, I positioned myself under her in case anyone had to perform a final check on the deceased. I was still for hours and heard the whole ceremony. Her mother poured her heart out about Marigold's wildness that was impossible not to love, and Felix spoke about the injustice of her being taken too soon. I tried not to cry in case someone heard me, including Marigold.

Finally, we were moving. The coffin bounced as it was carried to the car and then the final resting spot. Then came the fall. I felt us being lowered into the ground, no one aware of the stowaway soul in the box. We hit the ground and muffled words came from far above before I heard the dirt pile on. Handfuls at first and then the intense pouring from a dump truck. I should have been scared, but I was focused only on what I had to do to get my Marigold back. The darkness was complete, but I shuffled to my side, moving Marigold's stiff body to face mine. I placed our palms together. The ones that bore the scars from our ritual many years ago. I felt her. I felt her so much and I let my soul fill hers in return. We were as alive as we were dead. Together. Soulmates. Forever.

Outro

Content warnings: Teen death, murder, miscarriage (in outro),

A song that hurts my soul, *Pioneer to the Falls* by Interpol inspires this story. The song has been interpreted as the mourning of a miscarriage as well as a memorial to a murdered young woman. The latter is present in this story, though not based on any specific true crime. What gets to me about this song is how through the loss and grief, it never lets go of love. In particular, this lyric cuts me: "Show me the dirt pile and I will pray that the soul can take three stowaways." These were the first words lead singer Paul Banks crooned when I finally saw them at Reading in 2007 (I may have cried) and why I created two girls so tightly bonded that not even death can tear them apart.

These devoutly weird girls are also something of an ode to the Fitzgerald sisters from *Ginger Snaps*, my favorite movie of all time. In this case, neither of them is evolving into a monster, instead, they are surrounded by them in all shapes and forms. Men who do heinous things are so often labelled monsters. It works well as a metaphor in horror, and I struggled whether to use it or not because when it comes to real-life violence against women, it feels like an excuse. One that I don't want to perpetuate, but the monster-obsessed outsiders are who these girls became, and I wanted to be more faithful to them than any man.

Acknowledgements

I would like to thank everyone who encouraged me while putting this project together. It started as a joke inspired by an episode of the *Books in the Freezer* podcast where they recommended horror books based on Taylor Swift songs. So, I listened to Taylor Swift for the first time, heard the darkness in the beauty and declared that I would write a collection of short and scary stories based on her songs. That is not what happened because, around the same time, I read the book and watched the companion documentary *Meet Me In The Bathroom* by Lizzy Goodman, which chronicles the rise of the new New York indie sound circa 2001. The bands of this scene were my coming-of-age and soundtrack to those carefree uni days. I found myself wanting to write through and to the music that most represented my tastes and generational experiences, so it became a mixtape of millennial sounds and strange ode to the bands that I love. The way that these dark interpretations read may not seem like love, but it truly is the love language of my weird heart. Thank you for your music: The Strokes, Taylor Swift, Metric, Chvrches, Placebo, Sufjan Stevens, Mother Mother, Arctic Monkeys, Interpol, and The Smashing Pumpkins. These are by no means the only bands I wanted to pay homage to in these pages, but the stories you stirred in me sang the loudest.

Thank you to early and beta readers Craig, Nancy, Stacey, Steve, Ashley, and Phoenix. You superstars gave your valuable time, providing insights that transformed these texts for the better (and worse, where appropriate) and your encouraging words gave me the energy to keep hacking away at my terrible little tales.

A big shout out to Pearce Spiteri who came crashing into this process at the end and helped me be less afraid of putting myself and this book out there and inspiring all the marketing efforts. You have wild and unending ideas.

My dear friend and publisher, Andrea Cross, has my eternal appreciation for guiding me through this whole new world of publishing and having the faith in my work to put it under her indie imprint. You inspire me every day with your creativity and knowledge and I love your guts.

I must thank my partner, who supported me in every imaginable way through this project. I was getting over massive burnout from my last game and the process wound up being all-consuming—my ADHD knows no other way. Fortunately, this experience has been personally healing and validating, but I know my deep commitment to the book put a lot of strain on them as they picked up domestic slack and worried that I might backslide into burnout again. You are the most caring and generous person I know, and I am lucky to have you in my life.

Finally, thank you, dear reader, for buying this book. I hope it delights your dark places.

About the Author

Emily Flynn-Jones is an award-winning game writer and founder of the boutique indie game studio, Killjoy Games. She/They (hex the binary) has a Ph.D. in death, because why not?! A life-long horror fiend, they love how the genre engages with social and emotional issues just as much as when it's purely about making a bloody mess. When not writing, you'll find them playing games, thrifting for ugly things, or jamming out to eclectic beats. They also write queer erotic games for mobile apps and teach game design at a local university. A settler in Canada, they live with their partner and perfect pets.